Simon's temperature was definitely on the rise....

Along with other parts of him. How could he be walking wounded one minute and hyperaware of a beautiful woman the next?

The answer was simple, a five-letter word. *Megan.*

Insanity was the only explanation for his sudden, powerful urge to pull the nurse into his arms.

If she took his pulse, he wouldn't be able to hide his reaction to her. His heart was pounding, and she'd know it, too, as soon as she put her fingers on his wrist to take the reading. This whole thing was a bad idea. What had he been thinking to ask for her? He obviously hadn't been thinking. At least not with his head.

Why now? Why did he feel something? She'd made it clear she wanted nothing to do with him, which was fine and dandy because he didn't want anything to do with her, either—or did he?

Dear Reader,

Our resolution is to start the year with a bang in Silhouette Special Edition! And so we are featuring Peggy Webb's *The Accidental Princess*—our pick for this month's READERS' RING title. You'll want to use the riches in this romance to facilitate discussions with your friends and family! In this lively tale, a plain Jane agrees to be the local Dairy Princess and wins the heart of the bad-boy reporter who wants her story…among other things.

Next up, Sherryl Woods thrills her readers once again with the newest installment of THE DEVANEYS—*Michael's Discovery.* Follow this ex-navy SEAL hero as he struggles to heal from battle—and save himself from falling hard for his beautiful physical therapist! Pamela Toth's *Man Behind the Badge,* the third book in her popular WINCHESTER BRIDES miniseries, brings us another stunning hero in the form of a flirtatious sheriff, whose wild ways are numbered when he meets—and wants to rescue—a sweet, yet reclusive woman with a secret past. Talking about secrets, a doctor hero is stunned when he finds a baby—maybe even *his* baby—on the doorstep in Victoria Pade's *Maybe My Baby,* the second book in her BABY TIMES THREE miniseries. Add a feisty heroine to the mix, and you have an instant family.

Teresa Southwick delivers an unforgettable story in *Midnight, Moonlight & Miracles.* In it, a nurse feels a strong attraction to her handsome patient, yet she doesn't want him to discover the *real* connection between them. And Patricia Kay's *Annie and the Confirmed Bachelor* explores the blossoming love between a self-made millionaire and a woman who can't remember her past. Can their romance survive?

This month's lineup is packed with intrigue, passion, complex heroines and heroes who never give up. Keep your own resolution to live life romantically, with a treat from Silhouette Special Edition. Happy New Year, and happy reading!

Karen Taylor Richman
Senior Editor

Please address questions and book requests to:
Silhouette Reader Service
U.S.: 3010 Walden Ave., P.O. Box 1325, Buffalo, NY 14269
Canadian: P.O. Box 609, Fort Erie, Ont. L2A 5X3

Midnight, Moonlight & Miracles

TERESA SOUTHWICK

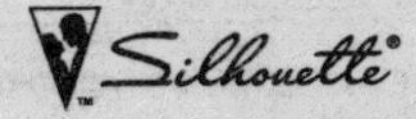

SPECIAL EDITION™

Published by Silhouette Books
America's Publisher of Contemporary Romance

For my editor, Karen Taylor Richman.
Thanks for giving me the opportunity to tell
this story. I hope I've done it well.

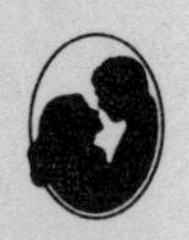

SILHOUETTE BOOKS

ISBN 0-373-24517-3

MIDNIGHT, MOONLIGHT & MIRACLES

This edition published by arrangement with Harlequin Books S.A.

Visit Silhouette at www.eHarlequin.com

Printed in U.S.A.

Books by Teresa Southwick

Silhouette Romance

Wedding Rings and Baby Things #1209
The Bachelor's Baby #1233
**A Vow, a Ring, a Baby Swing* #1349
The Way to a Cowboy's Heart #1383
**And Then He Kissed Me* #1405
**With a Little T.L.C.* #1421
The Acquired Bride #1474
**Secret Ingredient: Love* #1495
**The Last Marchetti Bachelor* #1513
***Crazy for Lovin' You* #1529
***This Kiss* #1541
***If You Don't Know by Now* #1560
***What If We Fall in Love?* #1572
Sky Full of Promise #1624

*The Marchetti Family
**Destiny, Texas

Silhouette Books

The Fortunes of Texas
Shotgun Vows

The Summer House
"Courting Cassandra"

Silhouette Special Edition

Midnight, Moonlight & Miracles #1517

TERESA SOUTHWICK

is a native Californian. Having lived with her husband of twenty-five-plus years and two handsome sons, she has been surrounded by heroes for a long time. Reading has been her passion since she was a girl. She couldn't be more delighted that her dream of writing full-time has come true. Her favorite things include: holding a baby, the fragrance of jasmine, walks on the beach, the patter of rain on the roof and, above all, happy endings.

Teresa has also written historical romance novels under the same name.

Dear Reader,

I'm thrilled to be part of Silhouette Special Edition. The books in this line have always been among my favorites, bringing me countless hours of laughter, tears and emotion-packed entertainment. It is with pleasure and a great sense of accomplishment that I join the ranks of these wonderful authors with the release of my first full-length Special Edition novel. It's a dream come true.

There are several people I'd like to thank for helping me turn my fantasy into fact. First, Susan Mallery, a talented and generous writer who also happens to be a dear friend. Susan always gives her support, encouragement and, especially, honesty. Second, my agent, Linda Kruger, for her organization, enthusiasm and determination. Third, Karen Taylor Richman, a terrific editor, who gave me this opportunity and also gives great ideas and expert guidance.

Finally, I'd like to thank you, the reader. In the end, your opinion matters most. I hope you enjoy reading this story as much as I enjoyed writing it. May you find *Midnight, Moonlight & Miracles* filled with laughter, tears and emotion.

Happy reading,

Teresa Southwick

Chapter One

Trauma team to the ER. Code three—ETA. Five minutes.

Megan Brightwell read the message on her beeper. Adrenaline pumped through her even as she looked at the turkey sandwich she'd just purchased from the hospital cafeteria. Code three meant paramedics were bringing someone in with lights and sirens—a possible life-threatening emergency. She grabbed the sandwich and raced from the cafeteria, turning right toward the emergency room.

Five minutes gave her three to wolf down food and one for indigestion. That left her just enough time to put on her I'm-too-cool-to-be-excited-about-being-on-the-trauma-team face.

Right on time the paramedics wheeled the patient in.

"Put him in trauma two," she said, glancing at the patient. A man. His eyes were closed, shirt torn and bloody, ditto the jeans.

The two EMTs did as instructed and, on her count, the three of them grabbed the sheet and transferred him to the hospital gurney.

"What have we got?" she asked.

"Motorcycle accident. Male. Mid-thirties. Normal vitals. Unconscious when we got to the scene. Witnesses said he tried to get up and his leg buckled. He woke up en route but keeps drifting in and out. Superficial scrapes, one nasty gash left shoulder. Bump on the head. Facial abrasions. We started an IV."

"Did he have ID on him?" she asked.

The paramedic handed over a wallet. "Simon Reynolds."

"Mr. Reynolds? Can you hear me?" She glanced at the man. His eyelids flickered and he groaned but didn't look at her. "Where's his helmet?"

"Wasn't wearing one," the EMT responded.

Shaking her head in disgust, she yanked her bandage scissors from her pocket. The blunt, angled end made it easier to cut away his tattered shirt and the bottom part of his pants. She grabbed a disposable razor and shaved five circular spots on his chest, then attached stickies for the leads that would hook him up to the heart monitor. The machine would take constant pulse, respiration and blood pressure.

"What have we got, Megan?" Dr. Sullivan hurried into the room and stood on the other side of the gurney, surveying the victim. He palpated the belly and then prodded, searching for evidence of internal injuries.

She filled him in on what the EMT had said.

"Take him to X-ray for a CT scan. We'll see what shows up. His vitals are normal, and it doesn't look like there's any bleeding in the belly. He just *looks* like hamburger."

"So he's not toast," she agreed, going with ER-speak for he looked a lot worse than he was.

"Probably not."

"Mr. Reynolds, I'm taking you to X-ray." His eyes flickered, but he didn't say anything.

Megan tugged on the end of the gurney, wheeling it out of the room and through the double doors for the short trip to radiology. Looking down at him, she sighed. "His guardian angel was working overtime tonight."

"Can you hear me, Mr. Reynolds? I want you to open your eyes now."

Simon decided maybe he would open his eyes if only to silence that bossy female voice. He wanted to tell her not to waste any more time and energy on him. He'd been aware of her—and other people—moving around him, doing X rays and bloodwork, beeping and poking and prodding. All their efforts were wasted on him, and it was time to tell her so. But when he looked up, a blond, blue-eyed knockout of an angel was staring back at him.

If he was dead, she was slumming. He'd already been living in hell. Dying would only make it official.

"Welcome back, sleeping beauty," she said.

"Isn't that the one where the wake-up call is a kiss?" He forced the words past what felt like gravel in his throat.

"I'm a nurse, not the fairy-tale police."

"Not an angel?" He remembered hearing something about a guardian angel.

She shook her head. "Not even close."

"Then I'm not dead?" A purely rhetorical question. The pain knifing through him was clear evidence that he was alive.

"You're still a member of the human race," she confirmed.

Maybe a member of the race. He wasn't so sure about the human part.

"Where am I?" He knew it was a hospital, but details were fuzzy.

"You're in the ER at Saint Joseph's. You're on a heart monitor, standard procedure for trauma patients." She glanced at the beeping machine beside him and the screen with lines spiking across it. "Next time you decide to give Evel Knievel a run for his money, I suggest you wear a helmet. Didn't you get the memo that protective headgear is the law? And it's designed for the purpose of preventing nasty goose eggs like the one you've got there."

Pain roared through his head like an Amtrak train. But still he lifted his arm to touch his forehead, and winced when he found a good-sized lump that confirmed her words. He noticed thin, clear tubing connected to his arm. An IV?

"Who are you?" he asked.

"My name is Megan Brightwell. Do you know who you are?"

"Simon Reynolds."

"Good. Do you know what day this is?"

He thought for a moment. When he remembered the date, consuming pain roared through him again, but this time it wasn't physical.

"Yeah. I know." He looked at her, wishing the protective haze hadn't cleared so fast. "You're a nurse? Then I guess goose egg is the correct medical terminology?"

"Actually, that would be contusion, but I didn't want

to get too technical with a man who just scrambled his brains.''

''What happened?''

''You don't remember?''

''Nothing except riding the bike.'' He shook his head, wincing as he instantly regretted the motion.

''I guess I don't have to tell you to lie still.'' In spite of her teasing words and tone, there was a sympathetic expression in her eyes.

The last thing he wanted, needed or deserved was her pity.

Metal scraped on metal as she dragged a privacy curtain halfway around the space where he was lying. Beyond it, he heard a phone ring and muted voices. Pretty quiet. The last time he'd been here all hell had broken loose. Must be a slow night. Good. Someone would look at him before his injuries had time to heal. He wanted the hell out of here.

''According to the paramedics who brought you in, one minute you were riding that motorcycle. The next you were playing slip and slide on the street—without the plastic mat.''

''The roads were slick.''

''Yeah,'' she allowed. ''Rain does that. And you just proved what everyone says—Southern Californians don't know how to drive on wet roads.''

''You're not going to cut me any slack, are you?''

''That's not my plan. Do the words 'slow down' mean anything to you?''

''And miss slip and slide?''

''Silly me. What was I thinking?'' she asked, her tone rife with sarcasm.

In spite of the stinging, throbbing and aching that encompassed every single cell and nerve ending of his body, he registered a flicker of respect for this woman's shoot-from-the-hip, call-a-spade-a-spade style.

He shifted on the hard gurney, then wished he hadn't. "I think I took a solid bounce or two."

"You have some nasty yet colorful lacerations and abrasions," she confirmed.

"Anything life threatening?"

"You almost sound like you're hoping." A frown puckered her smooth brow.

He shrugged and caught his breath at the pain that zinged him. "I just want to know when I can get out of here."

Except for that spot of worry between her brows, her skin was smooth and creamy. She was pretty. He couldn't be hurt too bad if he noticed.

"Is there someone we can call to let them know you're here? Your wife maybe?"

His chest tightened. "No."

"What about friends? Family?"

"My brother lives in Phoenix. Since I'm not dead, there's no reason to call him—or anyone else. Except maybe the doc so I can split."

"I'll let him know you're awake. He'll be in to talk to you as soon as he can."

"Can't you tell me what's up?"

"No. That's the doctor's job."

"Where is he? Playing golf?"

"After evaluating your vital signs, he ordered labs and X rays. While waiting for those, he went to see the other patient."

He remembered going through the tests. Then her words sank in.

"Other patient?" He frowned. "I didn't hit—I mean when I went down—was it just me?"

"As far as I know," she said, "that patient is medical as opposed to accident trauma. When we triaged the two of you, he drew the short straw. Doctor's been working on him for a while."

"If I came in second, I guess that means I'm going to live."

"You sound disappointed."

Maybe he was. She might look like an angel, but she didn't act like one. But then, how would he know? No self-respecting angel would or should give him the time of day. Even if he believed in them, which he didn't. Not anymore. Not since Marcus—

Suddenly exhausted, he closed his eyes.

"Stay with me, sleeping beauty." Her voice was sharp. "Mr. Reynolds? Can you hear me?"

Megan gently patted her patient's face and squeezed his hand, because it was one of the few places without abrasions. Probably because he'd worn leather gloves. What kind of idiot would protect his hands and not his head?

"An idiot with a death wish," she whispered to no one in particular. She gently patted his face again. "Oh, no you don't. Not on my watch."

"I'm not asleep. Who's an idiot?" he asked, opening his eyes.

She let out a relieved breath, grateful she'd easily roused him and he hadn't slipped into unconsciousness. "So you were playing possum."

"I don't play anything—"

Anymore.

The word hung in the air between them as clearly as if he'd said it out loud. She studied him. He wasn't hard on the eyes. In spite of the fact that he looked like the loser in a close encounter of the pavement kind, he was incredibly good-looking. But she couldn't help thinking he was in pain.

Duh. Of course he was. The man probably had a concussion. But she couldn't shake the feeling that she couldn't see where he was hurting the most. And since when did psychoanalyzing become part of emergency room protocol?

"No more pretending to be asleep, Mr. Reynolds."

"I wasn't pretending. And the name's Simon."

"It's going to be mud if you scare me like that again."

He grinned unexpectedly, chasing the shadows from his face, making him even more attractive. Her heart skipped, and she thought it was a good thing she wasn't hooked up to a monitor. With no evidence to the contrary, she could pretend she'd had no reaction to his smile.

Megan checked the machine and noted that his vital signs were all good. But the shadows in his eyes and the tension in his square jaw told her he was pretty uncomfortable. Unfortunately, because of the head injury, there wasn't anything she could do about it. Until the doctor assessed his tests and the extent of the damage, she couldn't give him pain meds.

But he was stoic. She couldn't help admiring that. And he was edgy. The cc or two of humor he'd injected into their short conversation gave her hope that his tests would come back negative, proving what she'd already observed. Simon Reynolds was strong and healthy. And handsome in a rough-and-tumble, rugged sort of way.

That was *not* a professional observation. It was purely personal, and she couldn't help it. She was a woman; she was breathing.

Short, wavy dark hair framed his face. His eyes were a vivid blue, a shade more intense than she'd ever seen before on anyone—man or woman. The thick, dark lashes were sinfully long and totally wasted on a man.

He looked like a fighter—lean and muscular. Now that he'd passed the golden hour, that precious sixty minutes when medical intervention made the difference between life and death, she could observe more details about him. Her haphazard surgery on his clothes had revealed a pretty impressive chest and strong legs dusted with a masculine covering of hair.

"So you think I'm an idiot, Nurse Nancy?"

She met his gaze, which, surprisingly, held humor. "I told you—my name is Megan. And while you weren't supposed to hear what I said, yes, I think you're an idiot. Kids know better than to ride a bike without a helmet. Unless you're a superhero I have to conclude that you don't have the common sense of a gnat."

"I hate helmet hair."

"Ah," she said, nodding. "So you're a vain idiot."

"Is it part of your job to insult your patients?"

"Nope. Just one of the perks."

"Are all the ER nurses like you?"

"Nope. They're worse. But then I'm fresh out of school. A newbie just filling in. I do four or five shifts a month to keep up my emergency room certification."

"Why's that?"

"I work for a home health-care company while I'm getting experience and waiting for a full-time position to open up here in the ER."

"Why?"

"I have a child. Emergency room nursing is highly skilled. The pay is better."

He flinched, then his face froze into an expressionless mask. As she observed him, the feeling hit her again that, in addition to his physical pain, he was stoic about his emotions.

Why did she keep doing that? Emotions had no place in ER medicine. Feelings were part of long-term recovery. For that matter, why had she just shared so many details about herself? She usually chatted with patients when she could, but didn't share personal information. What was so different about this particular patient?

"Megan?"

She looked over her shoulder and saw the ER unit secretary in the doorway. "Yes?"

"Dr. Sullivan said to show you this." The tall, thin, mid-fortyish woman handed her a computer printout. "He said to put it in the chart," she added before hurrying from the room.

Megan's eyebrows went up as she scanned the information. "Well, this is interesting."

"What's that?" he asked.

"It's procedure to check the computer for previous data on every admit."

"So I'm an admit." His gaze narrowed on her. "Would you like to share the information with me?"

"I suspect you already know what it says." She met his gaze squarely. "We saw you the first time a year and a half ago."

His forehead furrowed. "Broken ankle?"

"Skydiving," she confirmed. "Next was a shoulder separation."

"I think that was hang gliding. That tree came out of nowhere."

"Last but not least," she said, "a ruptured spleen—resulting in surgery."

"Waterskiing. I took the jump, and I remember soaring

through the air with the greatest of ease. After that it gets a little hazy. I think one of the skis torpedoed me.''

''It appears you're something of a regular here.''

She studied his pupils, watching for classic signs of concussion. The heart monitor would tell her his vitals, but she touched two fingers to the pulse in his wrist. For some reason, she felt the need to touch him.

''You have some dangerous hobbies, Simon.'' She met his gaze. ''Motorcycles? Hang gliders? Water skis, oh my. I'd say that makes you one of those guys who lives on the edge.''

''It's not a bad place to be.''

''Why?''

''It's the only safe place to feel anything.''

The words stunned Megan, but before she could respond, the doctor shoved aside the privacy curtain. The tall, balding, bespectacled physician had X-ray films in his hand.

''I see you're wide-awake now, Mr. Reynolds.'' He stood on the other side of the gurney.

''Thanks to Megan. She's keeping me on my toes—so to speak.''

Dr. Sullivan nodded knowingly. ''Megan's one of the good guys. I just wish she was full-time staff.'' He flipped through the pages of the chart in his hands, then looked at the man in the bed. ''Good news. Nothing's broken. But the paramedics who brought you in said witnesses told them you tried to get up after the accident and had trouble walking.''

''Yeah.'' His brow furrowed as he thought. ''I stood up and felt pain rip through my leg.''

''Where specifically?''

''Calf and thigh.''

"Since there are no broken bones, that would indicate soft tissue damage."

"You want to give it to me in English?"

"Sounds like muscles, ligaments or tendons. You'll wish it *was* a broken bone."

"What do you mean?"

"Bones knit fast. For everything else, recovery is painful and slow."

The patient nodded his head and started to sit up. "Okay. Thanks, Doc. Now I'll get the heck out of here so someone who really needs this bed can have it."

"Whoa." The doctor put a hand on Simon's chest and applied gentle but firm pressure, urging him back onto the bed.

Dr. Sullivan moved from the side to the foot of the gurney. "You're not seriously planning to walk out of here? And I use the term *walk* loosely, because if you've got the kind of damage I think you do, you're not going anywhere without crutches for a while. And the CT scan shows a possible concussion."

"Two-dimensional pictures of the goose egg," Megan translated, in case he didn't know the term from his other visits.

"You said *possible* concussion." He ignored her and directed the question to the ER doc.

"Yes. We need to watch you for signs of deterioration." The doctor looked at Megan. "Has he complained of nausea?"

"He hasn't complained about anything," she admitted.

Simon glanced back and forth between the two of them. "So we all agree I'm fine. It's been fun. I appreciate everything."

Megan slipped into a state of readiness when he sat up and swung his legs over the side of the gurney. He'd regained consciousness quickly, and his snappy verbal responses told her he was firing on all cylinders mentally. But the rest of him had taken a beating. At the very least, he had to be wobbly. If he started to go down, she wanted to be close enough to catch him.

She almost laughed out loud. At five feet two inches, a hundred and five pounds, her catching a big man like him was ridiculous. But at least she could break his fall, slow his descent so he wouldn't do more damage. She noticed the bright array of bruises, scrapes and one nasty-looking wound on his shoulder.

"You're in no condition to leave the hospital," she said.

"If one of you could call me a cab, I'll just be on my way." He looked from the doctor back to her.

"You've still got abrasions that need cleaning up and the laceration on your shoulder needs a couple of stitches," the doctor said. "If you'll just lie back down—"

"Thanks but no thanks."

Simon tore the leads off either side of his chest and the one in the center. Then he did the same thing to the ones on his legs. The sound of Velcro ripping followed as he forcefully removed the blood pressure cuff from his arm. Megan remembered that she'd had to find an adult large to accommodate his impressive biceps.

Inane thought. And one she didn't have time to analyze, because the idiot was going to leave without treatment. Before she could decide how to stop him or if she should even try, he removed the medical tape and IV from his arm. Blood dripping down the inside of his forearm mobilized her in a hurry.

She grabbed some gauze squares and pressed them against his skin to stanch the flow. Simon Reynolds must *really* hate hospitals. But in his condition it was the best place for him. She had a feeling rational arguments wouldn't get through to him.

"I say we let him go." She directed her comment to the doctor.

"I knew I liked you," Simon said with an approving smile.

Dr. Sullivan pushed his glasses farther up on his nose. "Megan, I don't think—"

"How far can he get? Between the leg and head injuries, it's just a matter of what takes him down first. The leg will probably buckle—if he can stand at all. He's pretty alert, but that bump on the head is bound to make him dizzy. Then there's the blood loss—" She shrugged and bent his arm up toward his chest to maintain pressure that would help stop the bleeding. "I have a dollar that says he bites the dust as soon as he puts weight on the leg."

"A whole buck?" Amusement chased the traces of pain from Simon's face. "You're not very sure of your diagnosis."

"If I had more money and a sucker around here who'd take the bet, I could clean up," she retorted. She glanced at the doctor. "We can just stand here and watch him pass out. Or on the off chance he makes it out of here, we can follow the blood trail."

"I thought nurses were supposed to be angels of mercy."

She looked back at him. "I told you I'm no angel."

"What about the mercy part?"

"Any moron who rides a motorcycle without a helmet, then tries to leave the hospital before he's physically ready doesn't deserve mercy."

Simon lifted one dark eyebrow. ''She's tough as nails, Doc,'' he said.

''I'm glad she got through to you. Now then, we'll clean you up and admit you—''

''I didn't say I'd changed my mind.''

Dr. Sullivan stared in disbelief. ''You can't be serious. A man in your condition—''

''I'm dead serious.'' He started to slide off the gurney.

''No,'' Megan cried. She hadn't expected him to call her bluff.

She instantly moved forward, insinuating herself between his legs to keep him on the gurney. For all her bravado, she was afraid he would hurt himself, do more damage than he'd already done.

When he slid down nudging her backward, she wedged her shoulder beneath his armpit and encircled his waist with her arm. He was heavy. She knew muscle weighed more than fat, and he had an abundance of one and no discernible trace of the other.

''Listen to reason,'' she ground out.

When he met her gaze, his own snapped with stubbornness. ''So it was an act? You're not going to let me fall or follow the blood trail?''

''Look, if you don't get the medical attention you need, you're going to be one gigantic infection and that will probably finish you off.''

''She's right, Mr. Reynolds.'' The doctor went to his other side and helped Megan get him back on the gurney.

''You can't keep me here if I don't choose to stay.''

''Of course we can,'' Megan said, bluffing again.

''Liar.'' Simon's forehead beaded with perspiration. ''I'm a regular. I know the rules.''

She looked at the ER doctor for help. ''Do something.''

"You know as well as I do that he's within his rights to refuse treatment. Is there anyone at home who can look after you?"

Simon shook his head. "I don't need anyone."

"You do need medical care." Dr. Sullivan rubbed a hand across the back of his neck.

"What kind of care?" Simon asked.

She met his gaze. "Stitches on the shoulder or you'll have the mother of all scars."

"Chicks love scars."

"Says who? And scars aren't the issue. But a nasty infection could ruin your day. The rest of your boo-boos need debriding."

"What's that?" he asked.

"You don't know? With all your experience, I assumed you'd be familiar with the procedure. But I see you're an equal opportunity catastrophe. Debriding is where I pick the gravel out while you bite on a stick."

One corner of his mouth lifted. "Way to make me want to stay," he said wryly.

"We'll give you a local anesthetic," the doctor explained. "But it's got to be done."

"Here?"

"Unless you sign yourself out AMA," Megan said. "Against medical advice," she translated. Although he probably already knew. "If you leave and fall down, you could hurt yourself even worse. But you'll have no legal recourse with the hospital."

"I'll risk it—"

"Why do you want to?" She put her hands on her hips. "Look, you gave us your insurance card, so I know you're covered."

"Money isn't a problem."

"Then what is the problem?" she demanded.

"I hate hospitals."

"*There's* a news flash."

"This isn't getting us anywhere." The doctor rubbed a hand across his forehead. "Look, Mr. Reynolds, what if you let us clean you up, then you spend the night here? We'd like to keep you twenty-four hours for observation, but we'll take what we can get. Tomorrow we'll send you on your way with a home health-care professional."

"A nurse?" he asked, looking at her.

"Definitely." The doctor nodded. "You'll need to have an IV, dressings changed, close observation in case of concussion. We don't want you passing out all by your lonesome. You're going to need general care because of the soreness. It's going to be hard to get around."

Simon was quiet for several moments. Megan could see he was thinking it over. Still, she wasn't prepared for his answer.

"Can I have Megan?"

Chapter Two

Simon figured if he hadn't already had his head examined, he would need to give it serious consideration in the near future. His thinking was crystal clear in spite of the goose egg. Although what he'd just asked sure didn't prove it. What in the world had possessed him to ask for Megan? The shocked look on her face said she wasn't keen on the idea, although there was no need to worry. He had no intention of actually going through with this home nursing thing. But her reaction made him damn curious.

She took one step away from the bed. "I'm afraid the home health-care system doesn't work that way, Mr. Reynolds."

"It's Simon, remember? And what way is that?"

"Assignments are handled by the coordinator, Pat Gautreau."

"What about requests?"

"It's not a call-in radio show," she snapped.

"I didn't mean to insinuate that it was."

"Time out." The doctor put his hand up. "I'm going to put in the paperwork requesting a home nurse for you, Mr. Reynolds. I'll get in touch with Pat and see what she can do to accommodate your personnel preferences. In the meantime, Megan, clean him up. One way or the other he's going to need that. I'll do the sutures when I come back."

"Yes, Doctor."

After the doc left, Simon watched her move around the small space. It took several moments to register that she never looked at him. She pulled over a stand-up metal tray and put a disposable cloth on it. Paper crackled as she assembled packaged squares, gauze and other mysterious packets. It looked like she was preparing for major surgery. If she pulled out a scalpel, he was outta there, even if he had to crawl.

Finally, she looked at him. "Okay, hero. Lie back down and grit your teeth."

He complied with her first request, sucking in a breath when every part of his body protested. He slowly let the air out, then said, "So why don't you want to come home with me?"

"What makes you think I don't?"

"My brains might be scrambled, but I'm not stupid." He watched her tear open a square white package, then closed his eyes. She was a bundle of energy, and it made his head hurt to watch her.

"I'm not sure what you mean." The clipped tone said she knew damn well.

"You looked like you'd swallowed a whole bottle of castor oil when I asked for you."

"Hold still. I'm going to spray on a topical anesthetic for the pain. It might sting a bit."

He felt something cool on his skin. It stung for an instant, then stopped and there was blessed relief as the throbbing discomfort went down a notch. He opened his eyes. "Come on, Megan. What's your deal?"

"I don't have a deal. You're imagining things. You should have your head examined."

"I already did. What happened to the straight-talking, take-no-prisoners angel of mercy?"

"I'm still here. Although you might have your doubts about the mercy part when I get through with you. This is going to hurt. I'll be as quick as I can." She let out a long breath, then said, "I'm sorry."

One minute he was thinking that her tone held heartfelt apology and he wasn't sure why. The next, fire shot through him and it was all he could do to hold it together. Sweat beaded on his brow, and he closed his eyes, concentrating on holding still. Simon gritted his teeth and clenched his jaw to keep from making any sound as she dabbed and prodded, rubbed and poked his skin to clean the scrapes.

Should he tell her not to bother? There was nothing she could do for what really ailed him. The wound was deep inside where no one could reach it.

"There. Done," she said.

He opened his eyes and saw her toss bloodstained gauze on the tray. "That wasn't so bad."

But he'd heard the raw edge to his voice. His scraped skin tingled and throbbed, hurting only slightly more than his throat from his effort to hold back any sound.

One of her eyebrows lifted. "Really? Maybe I missed something. I can check and see. Go through it again—"

"No!"

He met her gaze and saw the shadows in her wide blue eyes. Her lips turned up at the corners, evidence that she was teasing him. But it cost her. Every job had its downside. Hurting a patient, even to help, wasn't easy for her. Humor was her defense mechanism.

"You're absolutely sure?" she asked.

"Yeah." He let out a long breath. "I'm squeaky clean."

"At least your boo-boos are," she qualified. "Now I'm going to put on some antibiotic." She grabbed a packet and ripped off the edge, then squeezed until opaque ointment appeared. After touching a swab to the stuff, she applied it to his scrapes.

She met his gaze. "Okay, just a couple more spots on that pretty face of yours and you're almost ready for the doctor to suture your shoulder before you go upstairs for the night."

"You seem awfully cheerful at the prospect of passing me off."

"Really? And I thought I was being subtle."

"Why are you so anxious to get rid of me?" he asked, squirming.

"Hold still." She finished dabbing the ointment at a spot on his jaw, then met his gaze without blinking. "You're my worst nightmare."

"Wow. Don't sugarcoat it, Megan. Tell me how you really feel."

Her lips compressed into a straight line for a moment and she shook her head. "I can't believe I just said that."

"But you did. So come on. The least you can do is explain."

"No." She shook her head. "You're not going to provoke me into saying anything else."

"How unfair is that? I should get something for holding still while you tortured me."

One of her delicate eyebrows rose. "Now there's a switch. The person being tormented is usually the one who sings like a canary."

"I think it hurt you more than me. So give."

"No."

"Why? Why am I your worst nightmare?"

Still holding the swab, she looked at him, her eyes snapping. "Are you going to drop this?"

"No."

"Okay." She sighed. "You win. Why am I anxious to pass you off? You're dangerous, a loose cannon. Before you ask how I know this, I'll tell you. No one in their right mind would try to leave the hospital in your condition. Obviously, you thumb your nose at the rules."

"I prefer to think of it as marching to my own drum."

"You didn't bother to deny it. I have to admire that. But people like you are bad for me."

"Junk food is bad for you. I'm—"

"The saturated fat in the veins of my life." She dropped the used swab onto the tray beside her.

"Some son of a bitch dumped you."

"How did you know?" Her head snapped around so fast whiplash was a real possibility. "Never mind. We've already established that you're not stupid."

"That's the nicest thing you've ever said to me."

"It's probably the nicest thing I will ever say to you."

Simon found that bantering with her took his mind off the pain. There was no other explanation for the way he was acting, why he was pushing her—provoking her. If he didn't know better, he would call it flirting. But that was impossible. A guy only flirted to show interest in a woman, and he hadn't been interested for a really long time. Not in women—or anything else.

''So tell me about him—the jerk who dumped you.''

''It's none of your business.'' She picked up the empty packaging on the tray beside her, then toed open the metal trash can and dropped it in. ''I refuse to discuss that with you.''

''Come on, Megan.''

''It's unprofessional.''

''Isn't a nurse supposed to help with pain? Talking helps take my mind off it.''

She put a clean paper on the tray. ''Okay. We can discuss the weather. Sports. Movies. Books or—''

''I want to know about the creep who hurt you.''

''Why?'' She looked over his injuries, then met his gaze and smiled. ''Are you planning to beat him up for me?''

''Give me a little time. Seriously, how can I defend myself against being your worst nightmare if you don't talk to me?''

''For a guy with recent head trauma you're awfully stubborn, not to mention pushy.''

''And those are my good qualities.'' He studied her face, the shadows that chased away the sunshine.

''You remind me of him,'' she finally said.

''Go ahead—kick me when I'm down.''

''You insisted. Besides, I'm merely being objective—and truthful. He was a rule-breaker, too—probably still is, wherever he is. Good-looking—''

''You think I'm good-looking?''

''I didn't say that.''

''On the contrary, you said I remind you of him.''

''I was talking attitude not appearance,'' she retorted.

"So you think I'd have to sneak up on a glass of water?"

"I didn't say that, either." She positioned a nonstick square bandage on his left elbow. "Hold that."

He did as she asked. "So what are you saying? Am I good-looking or not?" And since when did he care whether or not a woman liked his looks?

"The average woman would not run screaming from any room you entered. There. I've fed your ego. Are you satisfied now?"

"So you would stick around if I came into a room?" He watched her cut strips of tape and place them over the bandage.

"I'm a pretty average woman," she answered with a shrug.

The backhanded compliment pleased him. He'd thought nothing and no one would ever do that again. "You're a long way from average, Megan. Which makes any guy who would walk out on you a first-class moron."

"Thanks." She smiled. "I choose to believe that, even though you don't know me from a rock."

"I know enough." He knew she was carrying around a fair amount of animosity. That had to mean she'd invested a fair amount of time and energy into the relationship. "I'm sorry your husband—"

"No way," she said vehemently. "Not my husband. I was stupid in so many ways, but at least I was smart enough not to marry him."

"Where there's fire, something's feeding it. What did he do?"

Her blue eyes darkened and her mouth thinned to a straight line before she answered. "When I needed him most, he walked out on me."

Her statement was simple and straightforward. But her

expression told him there was a whole lot she wasn't saying.

Why had she needed the jerk? No one knew better than he did that bad stuff happened to good people. What bad stuff had turned Megan's perfect world so upside down that the guy hadn't stuck around? Whatever had happened was still no excuse. A man didn't run out on the people who needed him.

He'd made that mistake once and the rest of his life was punishment for it.

"I'm sorry," he said, knowing the words were inadequate. He'd heard that until he was ready to scream. Sorry—five letters forming a polite response that made people feel better to say it, but hadn't ever done him a damn bit of good to hear.

"Me, too. But one good thing came out of it. He gave me my daughter."

A child—a girl. Crushing pain seized his chest. It wasn't physical, but felt as real as the injuries she'd just tended. From deep inside him, it rippled outward and settled around his heart. Marcus. His son. The best thing in his life. And he was gone.

Simon held still while she secured a bandage on his forearm. She looked at her handiwork and nodded with satisfaction. "Now we wait for the doctor to do your stitches."

"What do you suppose is keeping him? If he doesn't get back here soon—"

"What? You're going to dash out of here? You agreed to spend the night in the hospital and hire a home nurse," she accused.

"Technically, I never agreed to anything. But if you agree to be my nurse—"

"Even if I wanted to, I'm blocked off the schedule

until tomorrow afternoon. If you're set on getting out of here first thing in the morning, that's not going to work for you."

"Sleeping in to get your beauty rest?" If so, she didn't need it.

"Not a chance, hotshot. Bayleigh has a doctor's appointment."

"Who?"

"My daughter."

"Nothing serious, I hope."

She shook her head. "A checkup with her ophthalmologist."

"Can you reschedule?"

"I could. But I won't."

Before he could ask any more questions, the doctor returned.

"How are you doing, Mr. Reynolds?"

"Good as new, Doc."

"Glad to hear it." He pushed his wire-rimmed glasses farther up on his nose then looked at Megan. "Pat is on the phone at the desk. She wants to talk to you."

"Okay. And unless there's something else, it's time for me to punch out."

The doctor shook his head. "I don't need you for the stitches. Go home."

She nodded then walked to the foot of the gurney. "Good luck, Simon. Take care of yourself."

"Don't worry about me." She started to turn and he said, "Megan? Watch out for saturated fat."

She smiled, a beautiful wide smile, then she was gone. Instantly, he missed her—correction, he missed her sharp wit. For a while, it had taken the edge off his pain and emptiness. The two joined forces and closed in around him. The doctor talked as he injected a local anesthetic, but Simon didn't feel the prick or hear the words. He needed to get out of here. Megan was wrong—he was a stupid man.

A stupid man who *would* sign himself out AMA.

It had been a long night. When the sun finally came up, Simon reluctantly admitted that he'd been more stupid than usual. His body was like an orchestra's percussion section—throbbing, aching, stinging. And it repeated over and over. The slightest movement was agonizing, and he'd walked out without taking the prescription for pain medication the doctor had tried to give him. So he didn't move more than necessary. But now even he could see he needed help. He needed a nurse.

So he'd called the number on the card for Home Health that the ER doc had insisted he take with him. They'd sent someone right over. In five minutes he'd sized her up and realized she wouldn't do. She wasn't Megan. He'd called back and insisted they send Megan Brightwell—or no one at all. The consequences were theirs. Megan had told him she wasn't available until afternoon. He glanced at the clock on the living room wall. It was afternoon, and he was still waiting.

Leaning heavily on his crutches, Simon lowered himself onto his sofa. He clenched his jaw against the hammering pain as he carefully hoisted his Velcro-and-canvas-splinted leg up, then carefully swung it around and lowered it to the cushion. After letting out a long breath, he vowed never to take for granted the simple bodily function of going to the bathroom. He also made a mental note to decrease his liquid intake to just this side of dehydration so he wouldn't have to get up again anytime soon.

When the doorbell rang, he swore. "Come in," he called out, hoping it was Megan.

He watched the front door open and his visitor step onto the wooden floor in the entryway. "Simon?"

"Hi, Janet."

The attractive, fiftyish woman wearing designer jeans, tailored T-shirt and matching navy cardigan stood motionless, studying him from across the room. Her short blond hair was neatly arranged around her softly lined face. Her normally warm brown eyes stared at him in horror.

"Good Lord, Simon. What in the world have you done to yourself now? I came over because I was afraid of something like this." She slammed the door, then walked over to him.

"I don't want to talk about it, Jan."

"The fact that you're a mess from head to toe? Or that Marcus died two years ago yesterday?" She came farther into the room and stood by the couch, studying him. "Or do you not want to talk about the decision I was forced to make after the accident?"

"None of the above," he said, throwing his forearm across his eyes. But that didn't stop him from seeing the memories. "You've done your good deed for the day. You're off the hook."

"I was never on the hook. But okay."

For a moment he thought she'd listened and was going to leave him alone. But when she cleared her throat, he knew it was only the beginning.

"We won't talk about it now," she said. "But mark my words, the day is coming—soon."

"No, it's not. When are you going to give up on me?"

"Never."

"Why do you bother?" He removed his arm and looked at her. "I made your daughter miserable."

"It takes two people to make or break a relationship, Simon." She sighed and sat on the coffee table to face him. "Donna wasn't blameless. I'm afraid she had expectations that most men couldn't live up to. Now we'll never know if she might have found happiness," she added sadly.

"I still don't know why you waste your time on me. Surely you've got better things to do?"

"You didn't give up on me after I lost Hank."

"That was different."

"Oh? I loved and missed him. How is that different?"

"I don't have the strength to explain. It just *is*."

"You and Donna were divorced. But that didn't stop you from calling and coming by when I needed some chore or manly thing done around the house. Did you consider it a waste of time when you took me to lunch or dinner, giving me a reason to put on makeup and get out of the house? What about that line you fed me? That I was your son's grandmother and that made us family."

"It wasn't a line. You're a good person, Jan."

"And you're not?"

She knew the answer to that as well as he did. Why did they have to play twenty questions? He lowered his arm and met her sympathetic gaze. He didn't want or need her to tell him anything. Marcus had dibs on forgiveness, but he was gone and wasn't coming back.

"Don't think you're fooling me. I know what you're trying to do," he said.

Her mouth quirked. "What?"

"I invented the innocent act. It won't work on me. Have you been taking those classes again?"

"I'm sure I don't know what you mean."

"I'm sure you do. Those touchy-feely things you like. You know the ones I mean—Armchair Psychology. Ten Easy Steps to a Better Relationship, even with the former son-in-law who made your daughter's life a living hell."

"Oh, please. Don't be so dramatic. And don't scoff. Those classes are very informative and have made a big difference in my life."

"Have they helped you get over losing Marcus and Donna?"

"Nothing on earth can do that." The light in her eyes flickered, then was extinguished. "We both lost our only child. We share the same pain, Simon."

"Do we?"

"Maybe not. Mine is compounded. I lost my grandchild, too. It was a shattering loss. And I'm still trying to put myself back together. But we could help each other. I need to talk about it."

"I don't. And the last thing I want is help. Nothing will bring them back."

He wanted to recall the words as soon as they were out of his mouth. Her expression made him wince. She didn't deserve his abuse. He was very fond of her, but he wasn't fit company. He just didn't have enough reserves to play nice.

She stood. "Not that you care, but at least I'm trying to move forward with my life. You're living in perpetual midnight."

"What are you talking about?"

"Doom and gloom. Your new best friends. As much as I wished it was me who had died, I had to come to grips with the fact that it wasn't. Every day without them hurts like hell. But I put one foot in front of the other. You taught me that. And it takes courage. But I guess you've got more brains than guts. You talk the talk without walking the walk.'' She stared at his bum leg, then slung her purse over her shoulder and walked toward the door.

''Janet, I—''

She turned back and held up a finger to stop him. ''Don't say anything. I'm really ticked off. You lashed out on purpose to get rid of me. It worked. You hurt me, and I'm leaving. But that's not why I'd like to punch your lights out. You're wasting your life, Simon. I have no patience for waste.''

Maybe this time he'd finally gotten through to her. He wasn't worth her effort.

She took two steps, then pointed at him. ''And don't think for one minute you've gotten rid of me. I'm not through with you yet, buster. If it takes the rest of my life I'll keep after you. But I'm finished for today. I'll leave you alone now, since that's what you seem to want. But if there's any justice in this world and a god in heaven, each time you haul yourself up off that sofa, every muscle and nerve in your body will hurt like a son of a gun.''

Then she opened the door and slammed it after herself.

Simon let out a long breath. That certainly wasn't his finest hour. And he'd definitely gotten his wish. He was alone. Although he didn't feel a whole lot of satisfaction from it. If only the kitchen, the TV remote and everything else he needed could be within arm's reach.

In spite of the fact that he'd sworn not to consume liquid, he was so thirsty he couldn't stand it. Steeling himself for the pain, he pushed to a sitting position, then grabbed his crutches and stood. By the time he had accomplished that feat, he was sweating and dizzy. He'd held his breath against the discomfort he knew was coming and had forgotten to breathe.

The doorbell rang. Since he was already standing, he hobbled across the short distance to answer it. Maybe Janet had come back and he could make up for his churlish behavior. She reminded him of one tough, straight-talking ER nurse.

But when he opened the door, it wasn't his former mother-in-law standing there.

"Megan."

Chapter Three

Megan stared at the man with a death grip on his crutches and struggled to keep the shock from her expression. He looked terrible. Black, blue, and a rip-roaring case of the tired crankies. No, even more than that—tired clear to the bone. More than anything, she wanted to put her arms around him. The urge came suddenly and with such force it shocked her socks off. If she'd ever seen a soul in need of comfort, it was Simon Reynolds.

Hours had passed since she'd seen him through last night's emergency, but she still felt that somewhere, somehow, his soul had taken an even bigger hit. And she wanted to hold him and try to make it better. But she didn't. Gut instinct told her he was proud, stubborn and macho. He wouldn't take kindly to any comfort offered. Besides, she wouldn't treat him any differently than her other patients. She didn't make hugging a habit—unless they were children.

And he was definitely *not* a child. His wide, bare chest with the masculine sprinkling of hair testified to that. Last night in the ER it had been safe to acknowledge her attraction. She'd never expected to see him again. But here she was. Still attracted. Maybe more so. Her strong reaction to this particular patient convinced her that she needed to proceed with caution.

She retreated behind her trademark sassiness. "Hi, Simon."

"Megan. I wasn't sure you'd come."

"Pat's my friend. If I can save her the hassle of a nuisance malpractice suit—" She shrugged.

"I wouldn't have sued."

"We'll never know. I'm surprised you answered the door."

"Because you predicted I'd be flat on my back—if I made it home at all?"

"I thought you'd be out practicing for a world record in the walking-wounded Olympics."

"You just caught me. Another second or two and I'd have been out the door for a training hobble." His mouth turned up at the corners.

Unfortunately, it didn't make him look any less battered. Even more unfortunately, his words picked up where he'd left off last night—charming her.

Coming here was a really bad idea.

But the first nurse Pat had sent hadn't worked out and Megan had heard about his ultimatum. Her boss had coaxed and cajoled, then when all else failed, she'd brought out the big guns and called in a personal favor. Pat had given Megan a job when she'd desperately needed one. Megan had gratefully told her—if you ever need anything… So here she was, but with great personal misgivings.

She looked up at him—way up. ‘‘You’re a tall one,’’ she commented, the first words that came to mind.

‘‘I’m the same height I was last night.’’

‘‘But you were flat on your back then.’’

‘‘Until I jumped off the gurney and you propped me up,’’ he reminded her.

‘‘So I did. Although ‘jump’ is a pretty ambitious description.’’

She’d tried to put the encounter out of her mind and couldn’t, which meant she’d probably lost her mind. What she needed to do was look at this as an opportunity to sort out and put to bed the feelings he’d evoked.

Looking past him, she noticed the entryway floor was distressed wood. That suited Simon Reynolds, she thought wryly. She could see a stairway going up and one going down. The town house had three levels. And she knew it was a block from the Pacific Ocean. An expensive piece of real estate. His paperwork from previous admits had said he was an engineer. Apparently, it was a lucrative line of work.

‘‘May I come in?’’ she asked.

‘‘Sorry. I guess last night’s little spill has put me off my manners.’’ To let her pass in front of him, he started to back up on crutches he was quite obviously unaccustomed to navigating.

‘‘Don’t move,’’ she cautioned, fearing he would topple backward. ‘‘You get points for good intentions, but let’s save the backing up and parallel parking for another lesson. Until you get the hang of it, I suggest you move in a forward direction only.’’

‘‘You’ll get no argument from me.’’

‘‘Like I believe that.’’

Megan smiled. She couldn't help it. One minute, she was secure in the knowledge that her defenses were squarely in place; the next, he said something cute. The further she got into this opportunity, the worse it looked.

But she didn't have a choice so she simply moved past him. Close enough to feel the warmth of his body. If she hadn't been wearing a sweater against the cool November weather, her arm would have touched his—bare skin to bare skin. She was suddenly jittery. The close contact, his disarming grin—so attractive and so unexpected, the sheer masculinity of his unshaven jaw all combined to mobilize her hormones. If there was an antidote to his powerful appeal now was the time to take it. But she couldn't think of a single course of treatment to slow her reaction.

God help her—she was smack-dab in the devil's domain.

"Go sit down before you fall down," she ordered. "If that happens, no way can I scrape you off the floor by myself."

He winced at the words. "Falling's not high on my to-do list, either."

"What are you *really* doing up?"

She watched him hobble into the living room and slowly, carefully and painfully—if the tight, tension-filled look on his face was anything to go by—lower himself into the corner of his green-and-blue-plaid couch. He rested the crutches beside him, against the coordinating wing chair.

After letting out a long breath, he met her gaze. "I was thirsty."

She shook her head in exasperation. "This is exactly what the doctor was afraid of."

"Specifically?"

"Neglect."

Megan put her bag of medical supplies on the oak coffee table and left him sitting up on the couch. She walked through the town house dining room, past an ornately carved oak table and eight chairs, past the matching hutch and into the sunny kitchen. To her right was a circular dinette with four chairs. Behind it, in the corner, a bottled-water dispenser.

To her left was a long expanse of room with a refrigerator on the left, countertops and cupboards on the right. At the end was the stove and a built-in microwave. After pacing the distance of the room, she looked down the hall that led back to the living room. She noted the pantry and the powder room across from it, then retraced her steps. Taking a glass from the top cupboard closest to the water dispenser, she filled it and walked back to him.

"Here."

"Thanks."

He drank greedily, and she watched his Adam's apple move up and down. When he was finished, she couldn't help noticing the way drops of water clung to his firm, well-shaped lips. What would they feel like against her own?

Holy cow! Why should the perfectly ordinary sight of a man drinking water make her think about that, then go weak in the knees and steal the breath straight out of her lungs? There was a perfectly reasonable explanation. She was a ninny, of course. If researchers came up with an anti-ninny inoculation, she'd be first in line for human testing.

He held the glass out to her and she took it, mortified to see that her hand was shaking.

"I'll get you some more," she said, turning on her heel.

"That's okay. It was enough. I'll just have to—"

"Yes, I know. But your body needs hydration. If you were in the hospital, they'd slap an IV on you faster than you could say intravenous saline solution." She tossed the words over her shoulder on her way to the kitchen.

When she came back, she handed him the glass. "You'd also have a bedpan."

His intense, blue-eyed gaze captured her own. "Then my decision to leave was definitely the right one."

"Even though you'd have been more comfortable and better taken care of in the hospital?"

"Comfortable is a relative term. I'd have crawled to the facilities on my hands and knees before using a metal contraption you guys no doubt keep in the freezer."

"They're plastic. We haven't used metal bedpans *or* kept them in the freezer for years."

"Uh-huh. A likely story, but one I don't have to test since you're on my turf now. And I think my care quotient just went up."

The look he gave her heated her blood and sent it bubbling through her body. Unfortunately, she felt it in her cheeks, as well as other, more sensitive places. She hoped he wouldn't notice.

"Speaking of care, I need to take a look at you."

"You're looking at me."

She shook her head. "I mean I have to check your abrasions for infection. Examine the stitches. Etcetera."

"I don't like the sound of etcetera. Will it hurt?"

"No more than and-so-on-and-so-forth."

His blue eyes narrowed as he fixed her with a skeptical look. "You're lying. It's going to hurt. And me without a stick to bite on."

"I never lie. But I also didn't define how much discomfort is associated with and-so-on-and-so-forth."

"Okay. Lay it on me."

"I need to change the bandages. That will probably hurt some if there was oozing and they stuck. I'll have to clean the wounds again and put on ointment—as gently as I possibly can. Look on the bright side. I don't have to dig out the gravel."

"Lucky me. Do you always look on the bright side?"

"There's a reason my last name is Brightwell."

"Has anyone ever told you you're too perky?"

His twitching lips said he was teasing and took the sting from his words as surely as topical anesthetic. She was amused and charmed in equal parts. And there it was again. Heat. It started in her cheeks and gained intensity, turning into a fireball that shot straight to her toes.

She cleared her throat and turned to her bag. "After wound inspection, I need to take your vitals. A veteran like yourself probably already knows that means temperature, pulse and blood pressure."

"Okay. Then what?"

"If everything checks out, I plan to do some range-of-motion exercises on that injured leg."

"Whoa. Motion equals pain. No one said anything about intentional infliction of bodily harm. I called for a nurse because it's hard to flip a burger and stay upright on crutches at the same time."

She put her hands on her hips. "If you wanted a butler, you should have called Servants R Us. I'm a health-care professional. On my watch, you'll get expert health care. That includes making sure your nutritional intake is sufficient to support life for a man your size."

"Does that mean you'll do double duty as a cook?"

"Yes. But smile when you call me that." She allowed herself a quick, appreciative study of him and his impressive size. "It'll take a lot of food to keep you alive.

But I will cheerfully provide it since my primary function is to restore your health to pre-trauma status as quickly as possible. No pain, no gain.''

''I'll take the gain part and pass on the pain.''

''Unfortunately, they sometimes go hand in hand. Don't be a wimp,'' she challenged.

''It's not the pain I'm worried about.''

''Then what is it?'' she asked, unable to keep up the stern tone when his face took on a haggard look. She had a feeling he was no stranger to pain, and she wasn't thinking the physical kind. What was his story? No, she thought. Don't go there. Bonding wasn't her job. *Nursing* was—his body, not his soul.

But he was quiet for so long, she thought he might just tell her whatever it was that was bothering him. Instead, he looked at her and asked, ''How did your daughter's appointment go?''

''What?''

''You told me last night you weren't available this morning because she had an ophthalmology appointment.''

The man might have scrambled his brains less than twenty-four hours ago, but his powers of recall were annoyingly impressive.

''I didn't just fall off the turnip truck. You're not fooling me, mister. You're trying to distract me.''

''Is it working?'' he asked.

''What do you think?'' She half turned and reached into her medical bag for the blood pressure cuff and her stethoscope.

''I think I'm on a roll.''

''Since when are you a glass-is-half-full kind of guy?''

''Since I'm interested in what the doctor had to say about Bayleigh's eyes.''

"He said they're progressing normally."

He frowned. "What does *that* mean?"

A slip of the tongue. She hadn't meant to phrase it like that. Because she had no intention of telling him her daughter was a walking, talking, *seeing* medical miracle. That she'd had a cornea transplant and her progress was more than anyone had hoped for. That there was always the chance of rejection and every successful checkup was a blessed gift and a result of another family's devastating loss and incredibly generous, courageous sacrifice.

Simon Reynolds had his own demons to wrestle. He didn't need, or really want, she suspected, to know the latent anxiety Megan and Bayleigh lived with on a daily basis.

"The doctor said that everything is fine."

"Isn't she a little young for eye doctor exams?"

Megan shook her head. "She started kindergarten this year. It's for my peace of mind. I wear contacts and struggled with seeing the board in school and too shy to say anything."

"You? Shy?" The corners of his mouth curved up.

"What can I say? I've blossomed. Anyway, I wanted her to have a baseline guide so that if she begins to have problems in school, we can eliminate vision as the culprit."

"What a dedicated mom."

"And how would you know that she's on the young side for an eye exam?"

"I know a little something about kids."

Which was all Simon intended to say on the subject. Anything more would open up a painful wound that all her cleaning and ointment and taking vitals wouldn't help.

How he envied her. He also knew there was more to

her story. Her phrasing, quick backpedaling and the shadows in her blue eyes told him so. He guessed something about her daughter's health had sent her bonehead boyfriend running for cover. The idiot didn't know what he'd given up.

Simon would trade his own life if it would bring Marcus back. He would face health challenges or anything else for another chance to look into his son's smiling face, his sparkling, intelligent blue eyes.

But at the moment, another pair of big, beautiful blue eyes regarded him seriously. Megan. She was wearing shapeless pink cotton pants and a matching top that he knew were called scrubs. They looked more like pajamas. The idea gave him thoughts an injured man shouldn't be entertaining. How could she make the shapeless, sexless outfit look so damn sexy?

Megan cleared her throat. He'd noticed that was a habit of hers to get his attention. And a good thing for him that she did it. His train of thought was not only counterproductive, it was dangerous. He didn't want to care about anyone again. Caring and loss hurt more than anything he'd endured at the business end of Megan's healing hands.

"I'm going to take your temperature."

She sat down beside him and he could smell the sweet perfume of flowers, the innocence of a blooming meadow. Her hair was up, twisted into some sort of complicated braid. That left her long graceful neck bare. It was a beautiful neck.

"Open wide." She stuck the thermometer into his mouth. "Keep it under your tongue. It has to stay there for about a minute." She gave him a wry look. "In the hospital, they've got fancy gizmos that can do this in the blink of an eye."

He wasn't worried about time or inconvenience as much as he was that the darned thing would shoot off the scale. Because his temperature was definitely on the rise. Along with other parts of him. How could he be walking wounded one minute and hyperaware of a beautiful woman the next?

The answer was a simple five-letter word. Megan. Suddenly, he wanted to see another side of her, something besides the sensible, sarcastic smart aleck.

She pulled the thing out and read it. ''Ninety-eight point six. What do you know? Right on the button. Completely normal.''

''Don't I get points for that?''

''Let's do the blood pressure and pulse before we start negotiating for pats on the back, hotshot.''

She wrapped the black cuff around his upper arm and pressed the Velcro together to hold it in place. Pumping on the bulb, she inflated the contraption, then put the stethoscope in her ears with the flat, circular part on the inside of his elbow. The feel of her small, delicate fingers burned into his arm. He heard the slow whoosh of air as she released the pressure, and he watched her study the gauge.

When it was completely deflated, she ripped off the cuff and met his gaze. ''Hmm.''

''What is it?''

''One-twenty over eighty.''

''I've watched enough medical dramas to know that's right on the money.''

And he was relieved that it hadn't gone off the scale. The warmth of her body, the subtle scent of her perfume, the sight of her soft skin combined to make him feel that the reading might blow the hell out of the indicator gauge. Insanity was the only explanation for his sudden, powerful urge to pull her into his arms.

"Let's not do the dance of joy just yet," she cautioned. "There's still your pulse."

Uh-oh. If she took that, he wouldn't be able to hide his reaction to her. His heart was pounding, and she'd know it, too, as soon as she put her fingers on his wrist to take the reading. This whole thing was a bad idea. What had he been thinking to ask for her? Answer: he obviously hadn't been thinking. At least not with his head.

She took his forearm in her small hands and pressed two fingers to his wrist. He pulled back.

Meeting his gaze, she said, "You lose points for that."

"I'll chance it. As you can see, everything is in working order." And then some, he thought ruefully.

Why now? Why did he feel something? He'd trained himself when, where and how to let loose his feelings—when he was on the edge. And she'd made it clear she wanted nothing to do with him, which was fine and dandy, because he didn't want anything to do with her, either. His mistake had been not settling for another nurse. He had to get rid of her.

And he knew just how to do it.

Simon reached over and took her small, pointed chin in his hand. Leaning forward, he noted the startled look in her eyes, just before he lowered his mouth to hers. He tasted shock and surprise. Then, for several heart-stopping seconds, her full lips softened and he swore he heard the barest hint of a sigh. Obviously, he was wrong, because she broke the contact and jumped up.

She backed away several steps, as if he was fire and she was underbrush that hadn't seen rain in months.

"What in the world are you doing?" she asked, brushing the back of her hand across her mouth.

"I think that was pretty obvious."

"Why did you do that?"

"You're a beautiful woman. I lost my head."

"Not yet. But it can be arranged," she said, breathing hard.

"Look, Megan—"

Accusingly she pointed a finger at him. "No, you look. I don't know what your game is, but I'm not playing."

"It was no big deal."

"You're right about that. But it was also completely inappropriate."

"Nothing personal," he said.

"Doggone right. And I was right about you, too. Big-time rule-breaker."

"Don't get your stethoscope in a twist. I was just trying to shake you up."

"Is that so?" She glared at him. "It certainly confirms my assessment of you."

"That I'm the saturated fat in the veins of your life?"

"Right on, buster. But in case I didn't make myself clear, I don't play games. I came here to do a job and you just made it impossible for me to do that. I don't see signs of concussion—there's an understatement," she muttered.

"No, I'm pretty alert—"

"And your temp is normal," she said, ignoring his comment. She gathered up her medical paraphernalia and stuffed it into her leather bag. "I don't think there's any infection. At least not in your most recent wounds. And if you've got one somewhere else, there's not a darn thing I can do about it."

"What are you saying?"

"I hope for your sake the abrasions are clean because I'm outta here. I'll have the agency send someone else."

She turned on her heel and walked out the door.

Chapter Four

Megan slammed the door and stomped the length of the town house walkway, hurrying to the sidewalk. Her stride was just shy of a full-on run. The sun was warm, but a fog enveloped her. A fog that had nothing to do with being a block from the beach and everything to do with…anger? Or worse—passion?

No way. She'd deftly and *dispassionately* fended off advances from male patients before. She'd certainly never worked herself into a fog about any of them. She wanted to believe she'd handled the Simon situation in a professional manner, but she didn't buy the lie. Plain and simple: she'd lost it with Simon Reynolds. Everything: her temper, her composure, her objectivity, her professionalism—and that was the worst.

She'd gotten a late start in her career because of Bayleigh's medical problems. She couldn't afford mistakes now that she was on her way. What was it with Simon?

Oh, she knew he'd kissed her to scare her off. And it had worked. But not for the reason he thought. A come-on she could handle. It was herself she was worried about. She'd *liked* kissing him—far too much.

She didn't have to touch a hot stove more than once to know it hurt. After a crash and burn in the romance department, she knew guys like Simon should be avoided. If it was just her, she might be tempted. But Bayleigh came first. Megan wanted to give her a father, but the wrong man could scar her daughter more deeply than the trauma of cornea transplant surgery.

Nothing could compel Megan to take care of Simon. No amount of money, calling in personal favors or fear of a lawsuit could convince her to go back inside. Simon Reynolds was too tempting and too dangerous.

In her peripheral vision, Megan registered a car parallel-parking at the curb.

''Megan? Is that you?''

She turned and instantly recognized the woman getting out of the car. ''Janet.''

The older woman smiled, stepped onto the sidewalk then held her arms open for a hug. Megan easily slipped into the embrace and returned it. Janet Ward was the most loving, generous, courageous woman. When her daughter and grandson were mortally injured in a car accident, she'd made the decision to donate their organs for transplant. Thanks to her, Bayleigh had received the little boy's corneas and the gift of sight. After the operation, Megan had asked to meet the family and thank them. But the boy's father had refused.

Janet had graciously accepted Megan's gratitude in spite of her profound grief. Because Janet's loved ones were alive through the transplant recipients, she'd insisted on staying in touch with all of those who were open to the idea. Megan had a picture of her daughter with Janet in her wallet and knew the other woman carried Bayleigh's school picture in hers. And Janet had very carefully avoided personal references to the grandson she'd lost, not wanting to make Megan or Bayleigh feel anything but grateful for the miracle. They owed this woman so much more than it was possible to repay.

"What are you doing here?" Janet asked, then shook her head as she looked down at Megan's clothes. "The scrubs are a dead giveaway. You're working."

"I was. The patient is impossible." She smiled ruefully at her taller friend. "What are you doing here?"

"I'm here to see someone impossible, too." Something flickered in her eyes and an expression that looked like comprehension crossed the older woman's face. "Your difficult patient isn't a man, is he?"

"Yes."

"His name isn't Simon Reynolds by any chance?"

"How did you know?" Megan asked, surprised. "Since when did you become psychic?"

"Oh, Megan—" She put a hand to her chest and shook her head. "I can't believe this."

"What is it? Are you all right?"

"I'm fine." Janet glanced to her left and nodded toward a bench, the focal point of the corner and surrounded by landscaping that included flowers and bushes marking the entrance to the condominium complex. "Let's sit down for a minute. You might not need to, but I definitely do."

"Okay." Megan held her elbow.

Together they walked the several steps, then sat side by side on the wooden slats. Megan took a deep, bracing breath. The previous day's rain had washed the air clean and left behind a brilliant blue sky. In the distance she could hear waves from the Pacific Ocean crash against the shore. The only storm on her horizon had been Simon Reynolds, but he was behind her. Or was he? Megan had the strangest feeling that life as she knew it was about to change. Now who was getting psychic?

She looked at her friend. "What are you doing here, Janet? How do you know Simon?"

"He's my son-in-law. Ex, technically." She waited.

Megan felt the impact of those words wash over her in shock waves. "He's Marcus's father?" she whispered.

The precious little boy who'd donated his corneas to Bayleigh was Simon's son?

"Yes." Janet sighed and clutched her purse in her lap. "I was here a little while ago to check up on him."

"So you know about his motorcycle accident?" When the other woman nodded, she said, "But in the ER last night he said there was no one to notify. How did you find out?"

"I just knew." She laughed without humor. "It's not as twilight zone as it sounds. Marcus and Donna died two years ago yesterday. I had a bad feeling he would hurt himself."

Megan remembered his haunted look last night when he'd said he knew the date. Oh, God. "Are you saying he deliberately dumped his motorcycle?"

"No. Nothing like that. But since he lost them, he's been rash, reckless. It's as if he doesn't care."

"I gathered," Megan said. "His hospital rap sheet is proof of that."

"He takes chances without regard for his personal safety. I came by to check on him so I guess you could say I had an informed gut feeling."

"And he told you a nurse was coming," she said,

knowing the woman would have stayed with him otherwise.

Janet shook her head. "I told him off and left after he was abrasive and sarcastic."

"That sounds like him."

"But I felt guilty. He tried to hide it, but I know he's in a lot of pain. I didn't think he would allow anyone to nurse him. So I came back, armed for battle and prepared to bully him into accepting assistance." She met Megan's gaze. "How did you get involved?"

"I was doing a per diem shift in the ER last night when he was brought in."

"When is that hospital going to realize what a find you are and give you a full-time job where you really want to work?"

"Unlike you, I have no twilight zone moments, so I really can't say. But thanks for the vote of confidence." Megan sighed and pulled her sweater more closely around her when the breeze picked up. She thought back to the previous evening, which seemed a lifetime ago. "There's just something about Simon," she commented almost to herself.

"He's definitely serious hunk material," Janet commented.

"I wasn't talking about that," Megan said, but couldn't suppress a smile.

"So you agree with me."

"He wouldn't have to wear a paper bag over his head in public," she answered cautiously. "But that's not what I meant. Every emergency is different, but patients' reactions are similar. They want to know if they're going to be all right or if the injuries are life-threatening. He did all that, but there was a subtext to his questions. As if he was hoping for the worst. As if he didn't care whether he lived or died."

"I don't think he does. So he's still being impossible?"

"How did you know that?" Megan was distracted, still shaken by his kiss. He was impossible all right—impossibly attractive and appealing.

"You just told me. Is your shift over?"

Megan shook her head. "I walked out."

"But you've talked to me about dealing with difficult patients. To the best of my knowledge you've never given up on anyone. What happened?"

Janet's approving words troubled Megan. How could she tell the woman he'd kissed her and she'd liked it and that's why she couldn't stay?

"Sooner or later I was bound to run into a patient I couldn't manage. Simon was mine. He specifically asked for me, but—"

Janet reached out and gripped her arm. "He *asked* for you?"

"Yes. But I was crossed off the schedule because Bayleigh had an eye doctor appointment."

"How'd it go?" Janet asked, concerned.

"Perfect." A bubble of happiness expanded inside her then was promptly deflated by a pinprick of guilt. "Thanks to you and Marcus and excellent medical care."

"I'm so glad. She's a dear child." Her lips compressed as she nodded. "Now tell me more about Simon."

"There's not much to tell. He signed himself out last night against medical advice, but apparently thought better of it this morning because he called the agency to send over a nurse. Then he sent her packing and said they'd better get me. So here I am. Or was," she said ruefully. "I finally had to wave the white flag."

"Why? Does Simon know Bayleigh is the recipient of Marcus's corneas?"

"No. Until you just told me, I had no idea."

"Then I don't understand why you left him. I can't believe sarcasm sent you running. You're made of sterner stuff."

"It wasn't that." Megan twisted her fingers together in her lap. "He kissed me," she blurted out. Janet stared at her, stunned, and she hastened to add, "It's only because he was trying to get rid of me."

"Oh, Megan, that's wonderful."

"That he got rid of me?"

"Of course not." Janet clasped her hands together. "My goodness, this is his first hopeful sign since Marcus died. You have to go back in there."

Megan shook her head. "He deliberately drove me away."

"He's recuperating. He needs you. He needs help."

"I know that and you know that, but I don't think he got the memo. It might be best for him to suffer a bit and call the agency to send out another nurse."

"Oh, Megan, don't you see? He asked for you specifically. It's the first time since Marcus died that he's reached out at all. I thought his behavior more rude than necessary. It proves you got to him, and he doesn't like it one bit. You can't turn away now. You have to go back. It's fate, an unexplainable coincidence that brought the two of you together."

Her friend, and she did consider Janet a friend, stopped short of saying she owed Simon. But the thought was there between them like the proverbial elephant on the table. And she was right. Megan and Bayleigh owed Simon Reynolds more than they could ever repay. How could she turn her back?

But that kiss. How could she forget?

Megan figured she would just have to find a way. She sighed. ''When you're right, you're right. I do have to go back.''

''That's the spirit. Hippocratic oath, spread comfort, save lives and all that. Florence Nightingale had nothing on you.''

''It's not that, although my nurse's training will come in handy. He didn't want to meet with me two years ago, but he can't run away this time. At least he can't get very far very fast on those crutches. I finally have an opportunity to thank him.''

''No.'' Janet gripped her arm. ''You mustn't say anything.''

''Why not?''

''He's been shut down for two years, and I was beginning to think nothing and no one could get through to him. I tried being kind, then blunt and finally brutal. He lashes out and hurts back. That's why I left earlier. And I swore to him I wasn't giving up.'' She squeezed Megan's arm. ''But I was starting to and that's one reason I came back. For some reason he connected with you.''

''But he was married to your daughter. Doesn't it bother you?''

''He's been good to me.'' The other woman shook her head. ''He's a good man in spite of the fact he was wrong for my daughter. But if you tell him *your* daughter has Marcus's corneas, he'll shut down again.''

''Maybe he won't. Maybe he's ready to deal with it.''

''Don't ask me how I know. Maybe another informed gut instinct. But I just know if you tell him now that your daughter has Marcus's corneas, he'll give up. If that happens, I'm terribly afraid—'' Janet's brown eyes clouded with uncertainty.

"But if I go back in there and don't say anything, it will be a lie. I hate lies."

"I know you believe in being straightforward, and I love that about you. But sometimes brutal honesty isn't the best policy. I agree deception is wrong—in most cases. But not this time. It's been two years. His behavior really worries me, Megan. If he doesn't open up soon, I'm not sure he ever will."

"But how will keeping this secret help him?"

"In two years he hasn't let anyone in—not even me. And we share the same loss. I'm afraid you're his last chance. I think you can help him. And you've got some time. He can't run, and he can only hide if you let him or push him over the edge with information he's not quite ready for."

If only he hadn't kissed me, Megan thought. But if he hadn't, she wouldn't have walked out. Janet would have arrived and the truth would have come out right in front of him. How she wished that was the way it had gone down. Then she wouldn't be in this pickle. Between a rock and a hard place. She couldn't leave, and she couldn't lie.

"Okay, Janet. I'll go back. But I don't think I can keep my mouth shut."

The other woman nodded somberly. "I know you'll do the right thing, Megan."

"I'll do my best. That's all I can promise." They stood up and embraced.

Janet held her at arm's length and stared deep into her eyes. "I know you will. Give Bayleigh a hug for me and tell her I'll visit soon."

"I will. She's missed you."

"I've been busy volunteering at the hospital."

"I heard you're coordinating the organ donation program."

"They asked me to be a liaison between the doctors and the families who have so difficult a decision to make."

"It must be hard."

"Yes and no," she said a little sadly. "I've seen both sides. It's a unique perspective, and I try to be of help. But enough about me. You have a mission, and it's time to quit stalling and get to it."

"Who said I was stalling?"

"This is me, Megan. Now march," she said, pointing the way back up the sidewalk.

"Okay."

Megan turned away and started back. With every step, her heart pounded. She prayed for the right words to convey to Simon how very grateful she was to him. And she prayed for the strength to forget how that kiss had made her feel. She wondered which part of her would cooperate first—her mind or her body. Or neither.

Twenty minutes after Megan had stalked out, Simon was still sitting on the couch where she'd left him. He'd gotten what he'd wanted. He was alone. Would he have kissed her if he'd known that after she was gone he would feel like a man going under for the third time?

Not to mention the practical problems he hadn't thought through in his ill-conceived plan to keep her from knowing his reaction to her. He was still thirsty, still had to take care of his bodily functions. Then there was the more pressing fact that he hadn't eaten anything since... hell, he couldn't even remember. But it was more than hunger gnawing inside him. The gaping hole in his gut had grown bigger and emptier the moment the door had slammed. He hadn't felt this alone since losing his son. Normally, when this happened, he got on his motorcycle.

He shifted his leg and pain zinged from his ankle to his groin. That wasn't going to happen. "I can't even get to the john without being in a world of hurt," he said ruefully. "And now I'm talking to myself. This is just freakin' great."

He heard the knob turn on the front door just before it opened. "Ready or not here I come," said a familiar female voice.

Then Megan appeared in the doorway. And again he thought she looked like an angel. Backlit by sunlight, there was an aura around her that was both comforting, surreal and heavenly. He tried to shut down the gladness before it got a toehold.

"Did you forget something?" he asked.

"No."

"Darn. I must be slipping. Normally I have that effect on women."

"Okay," she said, closing the door. She'd nervously caught the corner of her top lip between her teeth as she moved farther into the room. She stopped in front of him and set her medical bag down on the coffee table. "Maybe I did forget something."

"What's that?" he asked, happy to see her in spite of himself. And if she grabbed whatever she forgot and headed back out the door—God help him. He didn't deserve any sunshine, but he couldn't help basking in her glow anyway. It was impossible to live in perpetual midnight with Megan around.

"I forgot the basic cornerstone of nursing."

"Which is?"

"To protect and serve."

"I thought that was the police."

"The same tenet holds true for nurses."

"I'm not buying it, Nurse Nancy. Why did you really come back?"

Now that she was closer, he could see the way her gaze left his for a moment. If it was anyone but Megan, he would think she was hiding something.

She hesitated for a moment, then said, "I know you're in a lot of pain both physically and—"

"Don't," he said harshly.

"What?"

"I don't need you to feel sorry for me. If that's why you came back, hit the road. I'm sure there's someone else who'd appreciate an invitation to your pity party. But not me."

"Because you don't need anyone."

"You got that right," he answered.

"That's not why I came back. I'm here because I remembered one of the first things I learned in nursing school and the message was repeated over and over in training."

"What's that?"

"Do no harm."

He laughed and realized he was actually amused. There was genuine humor in the sound, something he hadn't experienced in a long time. Not since—well, since meeting Megan.

"Do I need to remind you I was there when you were extracting the gravel?" he asked.

"Of course not. But sometimes you have to hurt someone to help them."

"Explain to me how that's doing no harm."

"You don't want to do anything to make a situation worse. Very often people will get better without intervention. When invasive procedures are the only option, it's important to do only what's necessary, and nothing that will make the condition worse."

"Okay. So how is abandoning me doing harm? I can take care of myself."

"I agree. But the effort it will cost you to do that will take energy that should go into the healing process."

He looked at her for several moments and finally said, "That makes sense."

"So you're not going to throw me out again, so to speak?"

"I'm not sure how I could do that," he said, nodding toward his leg propped up on the coffee table.

"I haven't known you long, Simon, but I've seen you're a resourceful man. Still I'm disappointed—that kiss was a cheap shot for a smart guy like you. Even a moron can kiss. But I feel I have to warn you."

"Okay."

"It will take more than cheap shots to get rid of me. It's my moral duty to see this assignment through."

"God is your co-pilot?"

She shook her head. "It's my obligation to spare some poor, innocent, unsuspecting home health-care professional from your cantankerous personality."

"Don't hold back, Megan. Tell me how you really feel."

The corners of her generous mouth curved upward. "I plan to stay for the long haul."

"Define 'long haul.'"

"Your insurance pays for an in-home nurse for two weeks. So I'll be here that long or until we banter each other to death, whichever comes first. If you really want to get rid of me, you're going to have to do better than that kiss."

His breath caught for a moment at the words. Memories of her soft lips, an even softer sigh and exquisitely smooth skin assaulted him. For a long time, he hadn't felt anything but the most basic human needs. Now needs of a male nature charged through him. He didn't want to want anyone in any way. But he also had no strength left to fight off the feeling of not wanting to be alone.

"Okay, warning noted. Now it's my turn. I may be injured, but I've got a lot more energy than you give me credit for. Are you sure you want to issue a challenge like that?"

"You call it a challenge. I see it as a statement of fact. Unless you're prepared to throw me out physically, I'm staying." She lifted her chin slightly, body language that could only be called stubborn.

"Then I guess we understand each other."

"I guess we do," she agreed.

His stomach rumbled, reminding him of his most pressing basic need. "Does doing no harm encompass feeding me?"

"It does." She started toward the kitchen. "Afterward, I'm going to change the dressing on your shoulder."

"The joys of the invalid are never ending."

She glanced over her shoulder and smiled, then continued into the other room. He heard the refrigerator door open, then several moments of silence.

"You're wrong about that challenge thing," she called out. "The real mission is finding something in here that qualifies as both nutritious and food. And don't even bring up the benefits of beer."

"The thought never entered my mind," he lied, unable to keep from grinning.

"We'll see how funny this is when you succumb to food deprivation."

From where he lounged on the sofa, he saw her drag the trash can across the kitchen. Then he heard the sound of things being tossed into it.

''This pizza is like cardboard and the cartons of Chinese food look like a high school science experiment exploded. I see a trip to the grocery store in my near future.''

''It can't be that bad.''

She peeked through the doorway. ''It can be and it is. But I've been known to work miracles with less.''

After she disappeared, pots and pans rattled and the noise of drawers and cupboard doors opening and closing drifted to him. A sensation stole over him that was rusty and unfamiliar. If he had to guess, he would call it contentment. But he had no right to it. He shifted his body, then sucked in a breath as discomfort shot through him. He closed his eyes against the pain—and the physical part was the easiest to bear.

He must have dozed, because the next thing he knew, a small hand on his shoulder shook him and he opened his eyes.

''Wake up, sleeping beauty. Your feast awaits.''

Blinking away sleep, he looked at the steaming plate on the coffee table.

''Let's make you more comfortable before trying to negotiate food,'' she said. Fluffing the couch pillows next to him, she said, ''Turn and put your leg up.''

He did as she instructed. Then she threw a dish towel over his middle and settled the plate on his abdomen.

''If you had an invalid tray this would be a lot easier,'' she said. ''I'll put it on the list.''

Simon eagerly eyed the omelette as his stomach growled and his mouth watered. ''Smells good.''

''It is good. Dig in.''

No one had to tell him twice. He didn't even recall buying the stuff. But apparently his shopping skills were on autopilot just like everything else in his life. She'd whipped up eggs, cheese, mushrooms and chives into a tasty culinary dish.

"Any possibility of a cup of coffee?" he asked.

"It's brewing as we speak."

As soon as she said it, he smelled the aroma wafting through his living room. "You're a magician."

"It's nice to be appreciated. Besides, I told you I could work miracles. Why would I lie?"

He noticed a funny look on her face just before he took a bite of the omelette. Then he didn't care why she looked funny as the light, fluffy eggs almost melted in his mouth.

"I most definitely appreciate you," he said, letting the understatement speak for itself. He was too busy wolfing down the rest of the food.

"I'll go see about that coffee," she said, turning toward the kitchen.

Her words were light and laced with satisfaction, but he noticed that once she'd settled him with the food, she maintained her distance. Bobbing and weaving like a prizefighter. Constant motion. She wasn't getting close. He wanted to smell the scent of her skin and the fragrance of her flowery perfume.

"Cream and sugar?" she called.

"Black," he answered.

"Good thing." She returned with a steaming mug in one hand. "There is no cream or sugar."

She managed to pass it to him without actually making contact. So she wasn't as tough as she talked. Her remark—you'll have to do better than that kiss—was nothing more than bravado. Either she didn't trust him, which was wise. Or she didn't trust herself not to make the same mistake with a man who reminded her of the jerk who had let her down.

He decided to see how far ''do no harm'' went. ''I think I'll let this cool off,'' he said, setting his mug on the coffee table. Beside it, he put his empty plate. ''Isn't it about time for etcetera and so-on-and-so-forth?''

A puzzled frown wrinkled her forehead. ''What are you talking about?''

''Wound inspection.'' It would be worth a little pain to see her get up close and try to pretend his kiss hadn't made a dent in her composure. There was a part of him hoping she would give him an opportunity to do better than that first kiss. ''Now that I'm fortified with food, I think I can handle whatever you throw at me.''

Chapter Five

The question was, could she?

He'd been to hell and back—no, not back yet. The idea of hurting him, no matter how unintentionally, knotted her stomach. This was the reason it wasn't a good idea to become personally involved with a patient. And she hadn't planned to. But Janet's words echoed in her mind. *You're his last chance.* So she'd kept the secret.

But Simon was right. It was time to change the bandages and check the stitches in his shoulder. That meant she had to get close enough to touch him. If only she hadn't said what she did about that kiss. She hadn't meant it to come out as a challenge. A man like Simon Reynolds didn't miss things like that and probably relished a dare. If she was going to follow through with this assignment, she'd have to watch what she said around him. No reason to give him further ammunition. He was dynamite without her help.

"Okay, then," he said. "Let's get it over with."

"Okay, then. Do you want to take a pain pill first?"

"I don't have any."

"Surely the doctor gave you a prescription for something in the ER. And probably an antibiotic."

"He wrote them."

"And you never had them filled," she guessed. "I'll do it for you."

Since he was stretched out and took up the entire width of the couch, she sat on the coffee table beside him. Studying him, she noticed a gleam in his eyes. It was far better than the hollow look of before even though she suspected he was up to something. Patients who'd suffered abrasions were content to be left alone. She'd never known one so anxious to have his wound probed. He *wanted* her to get in close, so he could shake her composure. Like she'd told him, the saturated fat in the veins of her life.

Two could play this game. And she was the one with all the sharp instruments. After pulling her medical bag closer, she retrieved her scissors. Despite her inclination to see his game and raise him a move or two, as slowly and gently as possible, she cut through the gauze holding the absorbent pad over his shoulder.

"Oh, sugar," she said, annoyed.

One corner of his mouth curved up. "You even swear sweet. What's wrong?" he asked, glancing sideways, straining to see.

"This nonstick pad is stuck like crazy glue." She met his gaze. "I'm going to have to pry it loose."

"No problem. Just rip it off quick."

She shook her head. "I don't want to pull the stitches out."

"Since when? If your bedside manner is anything to

go by, you would have seized the opportunity with gusto.''

''If I'd known you were—''

His narrowed gaze stopped her. ''What?''

She was going to say if she'd known he was grieving on the anniversary of his son's death, she would have been more sensitive. But she couldn't tell him that.

She hated secrets. She was a really bad liar. But she owed him. If she truly was his last chance, she had to learn to lie like a rug.

''If I'd known you were my next assignment, I'd have been an angel of mercy.''

''You said you're no angel and any moron who rides a motorcycle without a helmet doesn't deserve mercy.''

''For a man who had a probable concussion, your powers of recall are pretty impressive.'' He opened his mouth to say something and she stood up and leaned in close. ''Hold still. I'm going to ease this off.''

She lifted the edge of the Steri-Pad and slowly pried it up, millimeter by millimeter. It seemed like an eternity later when the square was free. ''In spite of the stitches, there was some bleeding, Simon. I'm sorry if I hurt you.''

''Real men don't feel pain,'' he said. But there was tension around his mouth and a muscle flexed in his jaw.

It was safer to look at his shoulder than the expression on his chiseled features. ''There's no swelling, oozing or redness. It looks normal.''

He glanced at it. ''I guess in your line of work, a shoulder laced up like an athletic shoe is normal.''

She caught her lip between her teeth rather than retort that nothing else about him was normal so why should his shoulder be any different. But she couldn't say that to him, either. Now that she knew.

''I see a lot of things in my line of work that the

average person doesn't.'' She noticed beads of sweat on his forehead and it was far from warm inside. ''Are you really okay?''

His blue eyes darkened as he stared at her chest just inches away. ''That does it,'' he said, annoyed.

''What?'' she asked, startled.

''I gave you a perfect opening for a zinger and you ignored it.'' His eyes narrowed suspiciously. ''Who are you and what have you done with Megan?''

''I have no idea what you're talking about.''

''Last night in the emergency room a tough-as-nails nurse named Megan Brightwell called me an idiot and a moron. She offered me a stick to bite down on and threatened to follow the blood trail if I signed myself out against advice.''

''So?'' She couldn't think of any other comeback. Whatever had made her think she could pull this off?

''You claim to be Megan and you look like her. But you seem sincerely remorseful about hurting me. That's not the Megan I know. And you haven't called me a single name since you walked back in here.''

Uh-oh. Was she really behaving differently? Duh, of course she was. She'd censored herself twice in as many minutes. Now what? She'd often heard the best defense was a strong offense. There'd never been a better time and she'd never had a more pressing reason to be offensive.

''Calling you names would be unprofessional.''

''You were a health-care professional last night and it didn't stop you. I might buy the act if you hadn't said you were sorry. And you called me Simon. Maybe the real Megan was abducted by aliens right outside my front door.''

"Don't be an—" She stopped and bit the inside of her lip.

"What? Idiot?" he said pointing. "That's what you were going to say. You've gone soft on me. What gives?"

"Nothing gives," she lied. "I would never deliberately inflict unnecessary pain, either physical or emotional, on a patient in my care."

"I liked you better when you didn't cut me any slack."

What she wouldn't give for a good case of selective amnesia. He expected a zinger from her and she let him have it. "And I liked you better when you were unconscious."

They stared at each other for several moments, then slowly a grin transformed his face. The dark look disappeared, replaced by an expression so charming, so flirty and teasing, so sexy. He was good-looking before. Now he was downright hunk-of-the-month material. Her breath caught, trapped in her throat. If he did that more often, she couldn't be held responsible for her reaction.

"Okay. Megan's back."

"Megan never left."

"Could have fooled me."

"Yeah, I could. Like taking candy from a baby." She forced herself to meet his gaze.

If he knew she was lying by keeping this secret, he wouldn't handle it well. She was sure of it. Her mission—and she'd had no choice but to accept it—was to help him recuperate physically from his latest brush with living on the edge. And to find out why he'd reached out to her of all people. If she could reach him, she had to do her best to heal his emotional wounds.

It was a daunting assignment, but maybe she could get him to choose life again. That meant she had to find the reserves necessary to fool him, even though it felt horribly dishonest. She had to tap into her well of sassiness to keep him from knowing the truth.

The wrong thing for the right reason.

"If I wasn't conscious, I'd miss all the fun," he said.

She raised one eyebrow. "Most people wouldn't define this as fun."

"I'm not most people."

"There's a news flash. Hold still, hotshot."

She used a swab to carefully clean the area around his stitches, then applied antibiotic ointment and bandaged him again.

He rotated his arm, testing the new covering and wincing a bit as he flexed his impressive muscles. Then he leveled his intense blue-eyed gaze on her. "Has it escaped your attention that you snap out the 'hold still' order when you don't want to talk about something?"

"That order is so I can do a decent bandage. It's darn hard to hit a moving target, in case you hadn't noticed. And just for the record, I welcome the opportunity to talk about you. We can beat the subject to a pulp if you'd like," she said, handing him his mug of coffee. "I think this is cool now. Tell me more about how you're not like most people."

But she already knew. Still, she had to find a way to get him to open up. He'd given her a small but distinct window of opportunity.

"Never mind."

"Oh, no you don't. You brought up the subject, it's not fair to abruptly shut it down."

"This is my house. I don't have to be fair."

Megan smiled. She couldn't help it. He was so like a petulant little boy.

He took a sip of his coffee, warily studying her over the rim of the cup. "What are you grinning at?"

"You." She cleared her throat. "I'm trying to have a conversation and you stonewalled me."

"So?"

"I make it a point to get to know my patients. You asked for me, you got me and that's my modus operandi."

"I love it when you talk dirty."

She sighed and shook her head at him. "Since you mentioned it, this *is* your house. You don't have pictures."

"What does that have to do with anything?" he countered.

"You said you're not like everyone else. I was merely agreeing. The people I know have personal photos and family pictures around. I don't see any here," she said, letting her glance swing to the corners of the living room and the bare tables. "Why is that?"

"If I said 'hold still,' would you change the subject?" he asked, sipping his coffee.

She shook her head. "Were you hatched under a cabbage leaf? Crawled out from under a rock? Created by spontaneous combustion? Left behind by aliens?"

"Would you like to translate? What are you really asking?"

"Do you have any family besides your brother in Phoenix?"

"How did you know about him?"

"You told me. In the ER."

"Right. When you asked if there was anyone to call. And the answer is yes. I have parents and they live there, too." He held out his empty coffee mug to her.

She took it and wrapped her hands around it. "Tell me about them."

"Keep this up and I'll show you how much better I can do than that kiss," he challenged, his blue eyes turning dark and dangerous.

"If you want me to leave, why don't you just ask?"

"If I did, would you go?"

"No."

"If I ask you to stop with the personal questions, would you?"

With all her heart she wanted to avoid personal. And to do that she would have to disregard his rugged, devil-may-care looks and his sharp, intelligent wit. She'd seen just a glimpse of charm and was eternally grateful. If he had any to spare and used it on her, she would be a goner. And how stupid would it be to fall for a guy who'd been hurt so deeply he had every reason to turn his back on emotional commitment? He *was* on the edge; obviously he didn't want to care about anyone.

Even if Janet was right and Megan could work a miracle and get through to him, he was the wrong man for her. The unbelievable coincidence tying them together made it out of the question. She would do her best to bring him back to the living as fast as possible. Before her emotions passed the point of no return.

She stood up. "All you had to do was say you don't want to talk about it."

"I believe I did in nearly every way I know."

Shrugging, she said, "I guess I missed it. Now, since your most immediate problems are taken care of, I have things to do before my shift is over."

"What kind of things?"

"I need to lay in supplies and make something for dinner that you can nuke. I'll try to make you comfortable, anticipate your needs. Unless you want me to get a night nurse—''

''No way.'' He shifted his position on the sofa as if the vehemence of his answer had somehow vibrated through him, producing pain. Then his gaze met hers, with a swift flash of vulnerability he probably didn't know was there. ''You'll be back tomorrow?''

She wanted to say no, but fate had taken that choice away from her. ''Yes.''

Early the next morning Simon swept aside the sheets Megan had put on the couch. Before she'd left the day before, she'd made up a bed there because it was easier than hauling his carcass up even half a flight of stairs to the master bedroom on the town house top level. It worked for him because there was a half bath on the main floor.

He settled himself and let out a long breath, tired already and he hadn't performed even half the daily personal care ritual he normally accomplished with hardly a second thought. If Megan hadn't prepared so much before ending her shift yesterday, he'd have needed that pain medication she got for him. The effort it took to care for himself was considerable. Energy she had said he would need to heal. Which was what had compelled her to return after he'd tried to get rid of her with that kiss.

Would she come back today? Anticipation hummed through him. She'd teased him yesterday about hospital care being more efficient than what she could provide. From his experiences, he knew there were sponge baths. Was there one in his future? A man could hope.

Hope.

There was a word he hadn't used in a long time. It

stretched and groaned inside him. How long had it been since he'd looked forward to anything? When he remembered, guilt crowded in. He had no right to hope. Marcus was gone. He would never be excited about anything ever again—a trip to an amusement park, learning how to drive, the nervous excitement before kissing a girl, making love, marriage. He would never have a child—a son.

Before Simon could descend lower into the familiar black pit of despair, he heard a key in the front door. It opened a crack before Megan called out, ''Ready or not here I come.''

Megan. She'd taken a key before leaving the day before. So he wouldn't have to get up and let her in. She didn't know peace eluded him day and night.

When the door swung wide, giving him an unobstructed view of her wide, bright smile and sparkling eyes, the most amazing thing happened. His miserable mood evaporated. It didn't stand a chance in the face of such formidable, unadulterated, cheerful, sunshiny perkiness.

''Hi,'' she said.

''Hi.''

''How are you today?''

How was he? God help him, he could almost do the dance of joy in spite of his bum leg he was so damned glad to see her. It was then he realized how much he'd dreaded that she wouldn't come back. She'd said she would, but no one knew better than he that you didn't always get what you wanted.

''I'm sore,'' he said.

''Tell me something I don't know.''

''More sore than yesterday.''

''That's not a surprise.''

"Those range of motion exercises are an invention of the devil."

She laughed. "It means they're working. You could be a good boy and take your medication."

He wasn't a boy and definitely not good. "That would be too easy. No pain, no gain."

"Right," she said. "Suffering the consequences of your actions and all that."

"I bet you're a good mom."

She stopped in the middle of removing her sweater and met his gaze. Almost guiltily, he thought. What in the world could an angel like Megan have to feel guilty about? He, on the other hand, had a Ph.D. in guilt and couldn't imagine she could know the first thing about it.

She hung her sweater on the stair rail. "I'd like to think I'm a good mom, but I just try to do the best I can. Have you eaten breakfast?"

He got the feeling she wanted to change the subject and had switched her trademark "hold still" for a food question. He was about to call her on it, then changed his mind. It was prying and that implied interest. He'd lost the right to be interested in anyone.

"No. Have you?"

"Yes. But I'll fix you something."

"Gruel?"

She stood on the other side of the coffee table and looked down at him, regarding him thoughtfully. Maybe sadly? "Because you're being punished for something?"

Well, wasn't she hitting awfully close to the mark. "No. Because you have a finely tuned capacity for healing and I figure you for a health-nut kind of person who believes in the restorative powers of gruel."

"Oatmeal professes to lower cholesterol," she shot back, her mouth twitching.

"Is it a talisman against a bad relationship? A way to

ward off jerks like me who are the saturated fat in the veins of your life?''

''What would you like to eat?'' she asked sweetly. Too sweetly if the raised eyebrow and spark in her blue eyes were anything to go by. Obviously, she planned to ignore the question.

''Eggs, ham, bacon or sausage. Or better yet, all three. Hash browns, biscuits. Coffee and juice.''

''Well, you hit one healthy food group.''

''Sausage?''

''Juice. Coming right up,'' she said, breezing into the kitchen.

Frustrated, he stared at the space where she'd been standing. Then he grabbed his crutches and hauled himself off the couch. Not because the emptiness Megan left in her wake got to him enough to brave the discomfort of a trip to the kitchen. He'd be damned if he'd let her get away with having the last word.

''What gives?'' he said. He stood in the doorway, letting his crutches bear the brunt of his weight. The view was worth the aggravation of moving, he thought, admiring her backside.

Bent at the waist, she was scoping out the contents of the refrigerator. She glanced at him, then pulled out food and straightened. After setting the items on the counter beside the cooktop, she said, ''I don't know what you mean.''

''You gave in without a fight. Are you planning to put me out of my misery by plying me with cholesterol then watching my arteries harden?''

''I thought this was what you wanted.''

''It is, but—''

She pulled a frying pan from the cupboard underneath the cooktop and turned on the burner before settling sausage links in the bottom of it. She angled toward him, a smile softening her mouth as she shook her head, bemused.

"What?" he asked.

"You're like a teenager who's begging for limits while at the same time claiming you don't need any."

Simon bristled at the comparison. A teenage boy was the last thing he wanted her to see. If he weren't on crutches he would show her the difference between a boy and a man. Then he remembered how well that kiss had gone over.

"So why are you fixing me what I want without a fight? And why did you buy all that heart-unhealthy stuff in the first place?"

"Because I had a feeling you were a heart-unhealthy kind of guy. And right now your body needs fuel and protein to heal. After that, you can deal with cholesterol issues. If you choose," she added.

"Why wouldn't I choose?"

"I didn't say you wouldn't."

"But you don't think I will?"

"Based on the fact that you don't even wear a helmet when riding a motorcycle? No."

He grinned suddenly. "There's the Megan I know and love."

She turned back to the pan as it started to sizzle and he missed her reaction to the word *love.* Why had he said it? Would his off-the-cuff remark scare her away like the kiss had? It was just an expression. She'd said, or almost said, the same thing to him, stopping short of the *L* word.

"Hey, hotshot," she said, tossing him a glance over her shoulder. "I'm already cooking. You don't have to flatter me into doing the dirty work. It's in my job description."

So he was just a job.

Good. His conscience was already full without adding

Megan to the list. He would only complicate things in her admittedly reluctant love life. She didn't need the likes of him mucking things up beyond recognition. And if he'd said any of that out loud, she would make some sarcastic remark about protesting too much. She would be right.

"You're looking awfully serious about something," she commented. "Let's table the cuisine debate and talk about something else."

Fine by him. "Like what?"

"Like why you don't have any family photographs?"

"I never said I don't have any."

"Not displayed," she pointed out.

"I'm not a picture-displaying sort of guy."

"Okay." She turned the meat in the pan and held the tongs over it as she glanced at him. "Tell me about your family. What's your brother's name? Are your parents retired? Did you grow up in Arizona? Are you going there for Thanksgiving?"

"Time out," he said, fitting the palm of one hand over the fingers of the other to form a *T*.

He didn't do holidays. Not since Marcus had died. How did she know the most painful things to ask? Was it the contact of that kiss? Did it give her some sort of insight into his subconscious? If so, and for reasons he didn't want to examine too closely, he wished he hadn't been stupid enough to kiss her.

"What's wrong?" she said, all innocence while studying him.

"Let me refresh your memory. Yesterday you said you would stop asking personal questions."

"Let me set the record straight." She held up the tongs like a teacher about to use visual aids. "I said if you wanted me to stop, you had to ask."

"I stand corrected. Would you stop asking personal questions?"

"No." She turned back to the stove.

"I'd like to trade one nosy home health-care worker for an abrasive ER nurse," he mumbled.

"What?"

"I said, why are you so nosy?"

She shrugged. "I told you. I like to get to know my patients."

"Why? Part of the curative process?"

"Don't knock it until you've tried it."

"I don't want to try it. The real question is how can I get you to stop the third degree?"

She removed the sausage from the pan and placed it on a plate covered with a paper towel. "Okay. You want me to stop? You've got to give me a little something."

"What?"

"One personal detail about yourself. Something to appease my natural curiosity and stop the questions."

"Promise?"

"It's got to be a good detail."

If she only knew there *were* no good details in his life. That wasn't true. There'd been Marcus. But he wasn't going to share that with her. He couldn't talk about his son. "Okay. I'm an engineer."

She glanced over her shoulder and gave him an "oh puhleeze" look. "C'mon. That was on your hospital records. My questions are stacking up and ready to spill over."

"I started my own company and sold it for a bundle."

She sighed as she picked up the pan and started to drain the grease into an empty soup can. "You call that a personal detail? I could find that out on my own if I chose to. I want a good detail."

"Define 'good.'"

Her brow furrowed and full lips pursed as she thought. ''You know. Juicy. Like were you married?''

''Why past tense?''

''This is me. Remember? If you were still married, I wouldn't be here to take care of you.''

''I could be separated.''

''Are you?''

He shifted his weight on the crutches as his arms started to ache. Something told him she wouldn't let up unless he told her the truth. ''Okay. You win. I *was* married.''

''Was?''

''She divorced me three years ago. That company I started was pretty successful and turned me into a workaholic. Gone all the time. Business trips. She was lonely and got tired of being ignored.''

''Simon, I'm s—''

''Don't, Megan.'' He heard the sharpness in his tone and almost regretted it. Almost. ''Is that juicy enough for you?''

''I believe it takes two people to make or break a relationship.''

''You don't know me.''

''I'm trying to,'' she said.

He met her gaze and despised what he suspected was pity on her face. If he didn't know better he'd swear she knew... But she couldn't.

''Look,'' he said. ''I told you something. Now it's your turn to share a secret.''

And that was when she dropped the hot skillet.

Chapter Six

Megan managed to dodge the hot pan and scalding grease she'd been draining. The next thing she knew Simon was there. Who knew a recently injured man on crutches could move so fast?

"Are you okay?" he asked, looking her over.

She glanced down. "Nothing worse than grease spots on my scrubs."

And a zinger to my conscience, she thought. He wanted her to tell a secret? Why had he phrased it that way? Did he know about Bayleigh's eyes? No way. He wasn't subtle. If he knew, she would know he knew.

"The pan slipped out of my hand. Just clumsy, I guess," she said, meeting his gaze.

"I'm glad you didn't get hit with the clumsy stick when you were picking gravel out of me," he said, his mouth turning up at the corners.

She snapped her fingers. "That's it."

"What?"

"My secret. I'm a kitchen klutz."

"A hanging offense if I ever heard one."

Megan's heart pounded and she couldn't tell if it was from dropping the pan, his wanting to know her secret, or—she very much feared it was number three—the fact that he was standing a mere two inches from her and she wished he was closer.

"Simon, don't take this the wrong way, but—"

"When you start out a request like that, it's a foregone conclusion that bad is going to be the only way to take it."

"Why don't you go sit down and elevate your leg?"

"Is that a medical directive or a personal request?"

"Both."

Dark-blue eyes gleamed with male satisfaction. "Do I make you nervous?"

"Yes."

"In a good way or bad?"

"I'm not going to answer that. Suffice it to say if you want a meal anytime soon, it's in your best interest to get out from underfoot."

"Yes, ma'am," he said, saluting smartly.

Megan grabbed paper towels to clean up the floor and heard the clump, click of his crutches as he left the room. At least while he needed them to move around, he couldn't sneak up on her. Letting out a cleansing breath, she closed her eyes for a moment. Fortunately, he didn't question the fact that her response to his question was flippant. Next time she would be ready when he asked her to reveal something about herself. And there *would* be a next time because she intended to chip away until he opened up. And she had no doubt he would give as good as he got.

He'd opened the door a crack and, when she made him open wider, she intended to stick her foot in so he couldn't slam it.

"So when are you going to give me my sponge bath?"

Megan looked up from the blood pressure gauge and met Simon's enigmatic gaze. He'd eaten breakfast then napped in spite of his stubborn protest that he wasn't tired, and now she was taking his vitals. The idea of a wash had occurred to her, but she'd been putting it off, hoping he was mobile enough to accomplish the task for himself. Or not bring it up.

"What makes you think you're entitled to one?" she asked.

"Because the whole concept behind *home* health care is receiving all the comforts of a hospital, including bed baths, on one's own turf."

Megan glanced at his chest. It was automatic, as if someone had said "Don't look" and of course nine out of ten people looked. In her precarious state of mind the worst thing she could do was look at this half-naked man who did things to her insides she didn't want done.

And why the heck wasn't he wearing a shirt? Injuries were no excuse. But she knew even if his chest was covered, the material wouldn't completely hide the wide shoulders and contour of powerful muscles that tapered to a flat stomach. What it *would* conceal was the masculine dusting of hair that made her want to touch him, to explore the male textures. How stupid and unprofessional was that?

"Do I pass muster?" There was laughter in his voice.

Megan was so surprised to hear humor she almost didn't mind that her cheeks flamed with embarrassment because he'd caught her staring. She wanted to deny it, but the secret she had was enough. She didn't want to burden an already overworked conscience.

She looked him straight in the eyes. "Just checking to see if the little circles I shaved on your chest are beginning to fill in yet."

"I thought you said you don't lie."

"I don't. And so I must admit I couldn't help noticing you're a fine specimen of a man."

"So is that a yes on the sponge bath?" One dark eyebrow rose, a challenge if she'd ever seen one.

Megan couldn't resist the bait. "You're not incapacitated, Mr. Reynolds. In fact you were on your feet watching me cook breakfast longer than it would take for a shower."

"What about the contraption on my leg?" he asked, lifting the limb covered by the canvas-and-Velcro brace.

"It's not a cast. You can remove it for certain activities."

His eyes glittered with a dare. "What activities might those be?"

"You know. Showers and—" Her face, just about back to normal temperature after he'd caught her looking, heated up again.

"And what, Megan? Are you blushing?" There was the barest hint of surprise in his voice.

"Of course not. I'm a nurse."

"I know. But your face is red. I didn't think nurses blushed."

"We don't. It's one of the rules. Like doing no harm."

He shook his head. "You're lying. But I give you points for trying to bluff."

"I'm not bluffing. Why would I blush? You're not my first patient. When you've seen one—"

"Seen one what?"

Heat crawled up her neck. Her cheeks felt as hot as the face of the sun. "When you've seen one naked man, you've seen them all."

"I'm surprised at you, Nurse Brightwell. That's so callous. Who knew you could be so unfeeling?"

If only that were true, she thought, wishing for nuclear winter. "It's true."

"You still haven't answered my question. Are you going to give me a sponge bath?"

"No."

"How come?"

There was the petulant little boy again. But if he were a boy, she wouldn't be between a rock and a hard place. "You need to be up and moving around."

"Didn't you say I need to conserve my energy and channel it into getting better?"

"I did, but—"

"Why did I know there was a 'but' coming?"

"*But* that's not a license to sit around and be a couch potato. You'll just get weaker."

He folded muscled arms over his chest, putting the lie to that statement. "Now I'm confused. Do I need to rest or to run a marathon?"

"You need to use common sense." She shook her head and threw up her hands. "Look who I'm talking to. I have a feeling you don't know the meaning of common sense."

"I have a feeling you're going to explain it to me."

"It's complicated, but an engineer like yourself should be able to get my drift. If you're tired, rest. If you're rested, move around until you get tired."

"And this is related to my sponge bath—how?"

"You had a nap. Nap equals rest. You should be able

to get up and hike the distance to the bathroom, take off the brace—''

''Along with my clothes,'' he said pointedly.

''Yes. Unless, of course, that's how you do your laundry. And take a shower.''

''I didn't think it would be so easy to make you blush.'' He shook his head as if he was bemused. ''Like falling off a log.''

''That would be your sphere of expertise, not mine.''

''Blushing?''

''Falling,'' she clarified. ''But you're really hammering this blushing thing into the ground.''

''Just pushing my advantage without mercy. Remember this the next time you gleefully extract gravel from my multiple abrasions.''

If she had anything to say about it, there wouldn't be a next time. Megan hated that he lived on the edge without regard for his well-being. She tried not to judge him, because she had no idea how she would cope if anything happened to her child. Even though Bayleigh's eyes would always be a source of concern, Megan would be eternally grateful for her daughter's gift of sight. But her life, her very existence in this world, had never been in question.

She believed if the inconceivable happened to Bayleigh, she would try to do her job to the best of her ability and struggle to find joy and a reason to go on—no matter how difficult. But Simon had stopped living and didn't seem to care if he died. The one juicy detail she'd coerced him into giving up had been about his divorce and being a workaholic.

When she'd tried to say she was sorry, he'd shut her out as if he didn't want to talk about it. Was the breakup of his marriage somehow involved in his devil-may-care attitude? He needed to voluntarily open up and Janet had convinced her that she was his last chance.

"Earth to Megan."

"Hmm?"

"You're looking very serious about something," he commented. "Is it my sponge bath?"

"You're like a dog who won't let loose of a favorite bone."

"Do you blame me?"

She pumped up the blood pressure cuff—tight. "You bet I do."

"Ow," he said, watching her take his pressure. "Give a wounded man a break."

"I would, if said wounded man deserved one." She ripped the cuff off and met his gaze.

"Yesterday you said a nurse's job is to do no harm. If I don't get help cleaning up, the health department will come in here and condemn me. That's pretty harmful."

She couldn't help smiling as she shook her head at him. "Outside of being temporarily sidelined by your leg, you're the furthest thing from a helpless man I've ever seen."

"But, Megan—"

"All right." She stood up. "I'll get everything ready. But there's only one reason I'm going to do this."

"And that would be?"

"Because you can't get those shoulder stitches wet." She couldn't believe she'd forgotten about that. Her only excuse was that she'd been distracted by his appeal. Which was why it wasn't a good idea to get personally involved with a patient.

Correction: she wasn't personally involved; their connection was purely coincidental. And she had a debt to pay.

"Now you're talking." He slid to the edge of the sofa. "How about if we do this in the bathroom so you don't have to cart all the stuff over here?"

"Okay," she agreed.

Simon wasn't sure why tormenting Megan was so appealing. Maybe the fact that while he noted the flush of her cheeks and searched for ways to freeze it in place, there wasn't room for painful memories. She was like anesthetic and the respite was heaven. He didn't deserve it, but that didn't stop him from eagerly pursuing it.

After following her into the three-quarter bath with pedestal sink and stall shower, he sat on the closed commode lid and let out a long breath. Every muscle in his body ached, even the ones he'd never been aware of before. He could have showered by himself. It would have been an effort, but definitely doable. Still, he was glad she'd caved. Having Megan involved in the process was a lot more interesting.

What had made her forget about the stitches? It was pretty basic that sutures had to stay dry. Maybe Megan Brightwell wasn't as immune to him as she pretended.

But she continued to pretend to ignore him as she assembled soap, towels and washcloth. After turning the water on in the sink, she sudsed up the cloth. The expression on her face told him she wanted to do this about as much as a stark-naked hike in the Mojave Desert.

"Okay, Simon," she said, grimly looking at him. "This is how it's going to be. I'm going to wash and rinse the big stuff. Then in the interest of discretion, I will step out and you can do everything else."

"Define 'big stuff.'" One corner of his mouth lifted when pink crept into her cheeks.

"Chest, back, arms, legs, feet," she snapped out without meeting his gaze.

"By contrast, that infers everything else is small. Therefore, I have to assume you find other parts of me...lacking?"

"I have no data on the subject. Therefore I'm not in a position to comment."

He would like to get her in a position to comment, he thought. The image caused stirrings he hadn't experienced in a while, at least not that he'd noticed. It was as if he saw a speck of daylight at the end of a long dark tunnel. Now that he did, he couldn't seem to turn away from the light.

"Nurse Brightwell, you mean to tell me when I was at your mercy in the emergency room you didn't peek?"

Her lips twitched, but she didn't laugh as she brushed the soapy washcloth over his chest and arms, carefully dabbing over the healing abrasions. "That would be unprofessional."

"Instead you harbor an erroneous assumption?"

"How would I know whether or not it's wrong?" she asked, deliberately not meeting his gaze.

"I could flash you. That would give you the necessary visual data to correct your conclusion. How about it?"

"No."

"Take your time. Think about it. I'm in no hurry," he said, as she washed his back. That was an understatement. She could keep that up all day and he wouldn't complain. He closed his eyes in ecstasy as she rinsed off the soap.

"There's nothing to think about. You're deliberately attempting to provoke me and I refuse to react to the stimuli." She removed his brace, then washed and rinsed the leg. After doing the same to the other one, she stood, soaped up the washcloth and set it in the sink. "It's all yours."

Sad but true, he thought.

Then she turned away, walked out and shut the door behind her. Simon sighed. Tomorrow was another day. And he found he could hardly wait.

"Mommy?"

Standing at the stove, Megan glanced over at her daughter. Bayleigh was sitting at the small dinette snuggled next to the tiny kitchen in their apartment. Sometime—out of nowhere—it struck Megan what a beautiful child Bayleigh was. Straight, shiny blond hair surrounded her face in a cute bob. Behind wire-rimmed glasses, huge blue eyes stared at her with all the normal expressions and reactions of a sighted child. How very lucky they were. Money was tight and a house of their own was on Megan's wish list, but they were together. And thanks to Simon's son, her daughter could see.

It had been five days since she'd learned of the extraordinary coincidence linking them. How could she reconcile the fact that one child had received a gift at the expense of another child's life? It wasn't fair. But how could she not be profoundly grateful for the miracle?

"What, Bay?" she asked tightly, her throat clogged with emotion as she whipped eggs, milk and pancake mix into batter.

"Can I have a pj day?"

On the rare occasions that there was an opportunity to be together with nothing to do, Bayleigh inevitably asked this question. After cornea transplant surgery, it had been imperative for the normally active child to stay quiet. Megan had come up with the idea of a pj day and talked up staying in pajamas, lounging in bed reading, listening to music and telling stories until Bayleigh had decided it was better than a trip to the toy store. Almost.

Thinking back, Megan remembered a nightmare. But now her life was perfect; Simon still lived the bad dream on a daily basis.

"You made me stay home from school," Bayleigh reminded her. "I wanted to go."

"I know you did," Megan said. "You would go seven days a week if they'd let you."

"I like school," the child said, a smile dispelling the solemn look on her small face. "But I like it when you're home, too."

Megan had asked her boss to find a substitute nurse for Simon so she could stay home. Bayleigh didn't have a fever, but considering the tough time she'd had as a baby and toddler, when cornea disease insidiously threatened her vision, overprotectiveness was a clear and present danger. And a constant struggle to balance. Besides, the poor kid had a runny nose and a cough that had kept her awake during the night.

Since school wasn't an option and Megan's mother was away at the family's beach place, today had seemed like a good day to stay home. Especially after dealing with Simon and his daily sponge baths. Not that Megan was a coward. No way. But memories of dragging the soapy washcloth over tan skin and corded muscle made her every bit as hot as his comments about taking off his clothes.

"Please, Mom. We haven't had a pj day in forever."

"No, we haven't. And that's the best offer I've had in a long time. Let's do it."

The little girl clapped her hands. "Can I have Mickey Mouse pancakes?"

Megan met her daughter's gaze as she stirred the batter. "Of course. That's how a pj day starts. Why don't you pick out the videos you want then hop in bed? I'll bring breakfast as soon as it's ready.''

''Ya-ay.'' Bayleigh hopped down from her chair and went to the entertainment center in the living room.

Megan could hear her child going through their movie library as she dropped batter into three connected circles on the heated griddle. When the mouse shape was cooked on both sides, she used strawberries and whipped cream to make eyes, nose and mouth. After pouring juice, she arranged everything on a tray and carried it into the bedroom where the little girl waited.

Megan's room was large enough to accommodate her queen-size bed, matching dresser and computer desk with enough space left over to move around easily. There was a walk-in closet to her left and a bath beside it. Bayleigh's room was right next door.

The little girl, wearing flannel pajamas sporting the likenesses of her favorite television superheroines, reclined in the center of the big bed. Propped up by a mound of pillows, she wielded the remote control like a royal scepter.

''Breakfast is served, Your Majesty.''

''Oh, Mommy. You're silly.''

''Good. That's the way I'm supposed to be on a pj day.''

Megan settled the tray on her daughter's lap. After allowing Bayleigh to wrestle with the pancakes for a moment, Megan finally reached over and cut it into pieces. Bayleigh ate without talking for several moments while Megan quietly sipped her coffee.

''Oh, no. Mommy, I just remembered,'' she finally said, a dramatic note to her voice.

''What?''

''It was my day to bring Lucky home.''

Now an experienced kindergarten mom, Megan knew that Lucky was a stuffed bear who went home with a different student every day. He was to be treated like a member of the family and the assignment was to tell a story about what the bear did. Bayleigh had been anxious for her next turn.

"I'm sorry, sweetie. Maybe Mrs. Coates will let you bring Lucky home when you go back to school."

"Maybe. Hannah's after me. Maybe we can trade turns."

"Maybe."

"That means Lucky will have to go to soccer practice with her."

"I'm sure Lucky won't mind."

"How come you wouldn't let me play soccer with Hannah?"

"Maybe next year," Megan said quickly.

Once Bayleigh's eyes had healed and showed no sign of rejecting the corneas, the doctor had said Bayleigh could do anything she wanted. But Megan had never gotten over the warning right after surgery about avoiding activities that could result in a direct blow to the eyes. She wasn't keen on the idea of Bay taking a ball in the face or the jarring of running up and down the field.

"Hannah says it's fun," Bayleigh persisted.

"I'm glad."

"Her dad is the coach."

"That's nice," she answered, stomach knotting. She braced herself for the question that always came next.

"Where's my dad?"

"I don't know, Bay. I haven't heard from him in a long time."

"Since after I was born? 'Cuz he was scared about my eyes?"

"That's right. He didn't know how to help when he knew you couldn't see. That hurt him." It had been five years and Megan still struggled to keep the anger out of her voice.

"I can see now."

"Yes, you can." And how could she explain that she'd contacted Bay's dad to let him know the surgery had been successful, but he'd said he still couldn't handle it? Megan could have made a legal stink about child support but figured if he didn't want to be there, she and Bayleigh didn't want or need him—or anything from him. But she couldn't shake her guilt for getting mixed up with the loser in the first place.

"It's you and me against the world, kiddo. We're enough for each other, aren't we?" she asked, slipping an arm around her child's small, slender shoulders and pulling her close.

"I love you so much, Mommy."

"I love you, too, sweetie."

She didn't miss the fact that Bayleigh hadn't answered the question or gone out of her way to inflict guilt. Because of course Megan wasn't enough. Every child needed and deserved a mother and a father. She'd had her sister Cassie, her brother Dan and two parents who loved them. Megan's fondest wish had always been to give her daughter the same stability and security she'd enjoyed growing up. A perfect family, a perfect life.

And what a terrific job she'd done, she thought sadly. The man who should have loved, supported and protected their little girl had split at the first sign of trouble. Megan couldn't tell her daughter that he just didn't want either of them. So much for perfect.

Her thoughts strayed to Simon. Now there was a man who loved his child. So much that the idea of moving on without his son was too painful to bear, causing him to shut down. She would bet he'd been a terrific father.

Whoa, nellie!

That was a minefield and a place she so didn't want to go. The fact that Megan was attracted to the man was irrelevant. She'd allowed her heart to lead her with Bayleigh's father, and he'd showed his lack of a spine when the going got rough. If she ever decided to take a chance on romance, she would definitely lead with her head. Megan already knew Simon's story, and it was a beaut. Under the circumstances, letting such a flawed man into their lives would be a mistake of monumental proportions.

The phone rang and Bayleigh was on the side of the bed closest to it. Megan started to reach across her.

"No. Let me answer it, Mommy. Please?"

Because Bay always asked, they had been working on phone etiquette. "Okay. Remember what you're supposed to say?"

The child tilted her head and gave her a droll expression. "I'm in kindergarten, Mom."

"'Nuff said." Megan lifted the tray from her daughter's lap, then turned away to hide her smile.

On the third ring, Bayleigh lifted the receiver from its cradle. "Brightwell res'dence. This is Bayleigh. Who's this?"

Megan winced. The script was supposed to read, "May I ask who's calling?"

She listened then said, "I'm sick today, and Grammy's at the beach. I wanted to go to school, but Mommy wouldn't let me. Who are you?" She stayed quiet, then asked, "How do you know my mommy?"

The caller must have asked what she was doing, because the response was, ''Mommy and me are having a pj day.''

So much for all the training about not answering questions.

The child listened solemnly for a moment, then responded, ''It's when we watch videos, read books and tell stories all day in bed in our pajamas.''

Bayleigh listened again, nodding. ''Okay.'' She handed the cordless receiver over and said loudly, ''Simon says I gotta give you the phone.''

Chapter Seven

"Simon says? I like that."

The familiar deep voice sent hot flashes and cold chills up and down Megan's spine. Tension knotted in her belly, an indication that they didn't even have to be in the same room for him to affect her. "Why?"

"It means I can make you do anything I want as long as I say 'Simon says.'"

The seductive tone conveyed the anything he meant had to do with tangled sheets and bare skin. Cravings of a sexual nature shot straight through the thawing senses she kept in the deep freeze. "That's game-playing and only a notch or two above rule-breaking in my book."

"What's wrong, Mommy? Are you mad? He sounds nice."

Megan looked into her child's eyes. Simon probably was nice, but not for Bayleigh. Or herself. "He's Mommy's patient, sweetie."

"Oh." She thought for a moment. "What's the matter with him?"

"Don't even think about telling her I need to have my head examined," Simon advised.

"I wouldn't dream of it. But my daughter and I need to work on her voice volume control," she answered into the receiver. She met Bayleigh's gaze and said, "Sweetie, Simon had an accident. His leg is hurt, and he has to use crutches."

The little girl's face lit up like the town square at Christmas. "I know. I'm going to make him a picture," she said, scrambling out of the bed. "So he'll feel better."

"Good idea, sweetie." Megan watched her race from the room. She put the phone back up to her ear. "How did you get my home number?"

"Would you believe charm?"

"About as much as I'd believe you're able to leap tall buildings in a single bound—in your current condition. Speaking of that—how's every *little* thing?"

"There's the zinger." A deep chuckle from the other end of the line came through loud and clear. "Now that I've had my daily dose of abuse, can we talk about why you sent the Swedish Mangler to take care of me?"

"Not until you tell me how you got this number."

"Information."

"I'm not supposed to be listed."

"I'll be sure and pass that along to the information operator."

In spite of her misgivings, just hearing his voice gave Megan's spirits a shot of adrenaline and she couldn't find the will to be mad at the phone company's mistake. Until that moment, she hadn't realized she'd missed seeing him.

"So Bayleigh's sick?" he asked.

"Don't try to distract me. I'm mad at you."

"No, you're not. Tell me what's wrong with her."

Wishing she were a better actress, Megan sighed. "A cold. She has a goopy nose and a cough that sounds more like a barking seal than an actual barking seal."

"Goopy? That would be the correct medical term?"

"It would." She couldn't help smiling, but tried to keep it out of her voice when she asked, "What do you want, Simon?"

"I wanted to let you know that your replacement finished off what was left of my leg with her range-of-motion exercises."

"You're exaggerating."

"Possibly," he admitted. "I just called to make sure you're all right."

"Aha. I know what you're up to."

"Really? That would be a real trick since I'm not up to anything."

"Ooh, I can picture the innocent expression on your face. You wanted to make sure I'm coming back tomorrow."

"Are you?" he asked, his tone edgy and expectant.

"Yes. Even if Bayleigh's still under the weather, my mom will be home. So, God willing and the creek don't rise, I will be back tomorrow. How sweet of you to care."

"I'm a lot of things, Megan. But sweet isn't one of them. Selfish maybe."

"How can you say that? You want me back."

"It's more a case of the bad you know is better than the bad you don't."

Megan heaved an exaggerated sigh. "And here I was beginning to think you cared."

''You know what your problem is?''

''Yes.''

''No, you don't. Your problem is you think too much. Hang on.'' His voice was muted as he spoke to someone. ''Listen, I have to go. But I have just two things to say.''

''Okay. Number one?''

''If you don't have child care, you can bring said child along with you.''

Stunned didn't begin to describe Megan's feelings. Either her replacement really was a Frau Blucher clone or—Simon Reynolds had just made a major breakthrough. Permission to bring a child into his world? Did he really know what he was saying or had the ''Swedish Mangler'' done a tap dance on his head?

She hoped it was another positive sign—the first being that he'd taken the time and trouble to track down her phone number in the first place.

''Okay. What's the second thing?'' she asked.

''Tomorrow, I want a pj day.''

''I've seen your wardrobe. You don't own pj's.''

''But we can still read, watch videos and tell stories. In bed.''

Before Megan could retort, there was a click on the other end of the line. Staring at the receiver in her hand as if it were a particularly creepy reptile, she realized Simon Reynolds had just come on to her.

How did she feel about that? Her pounding heart, sweaty palms and total giddiness were a big clue. As soon as she could manage to engage her brain sufficiently to override her visceral reaction, everything would be fine. But how was she going to make that happen?

Her female feelings were coming to life. The feelings of a woman who hadn't been with a man for a very, very long time. Partly because she hadn't met anyone who piqued her interest. Mostly because she couldn't afford to make a mistake with the wrong man. Then along came Simon, who was definitely wrong.

She couldn't worry about that. Instead she chose to focus on the fact that he'd issued an open invitation to a child. Definitely a hopeful sign, and none too soon. His phone appeal was just as powerful as his face-to-face—or mouth-to-mouth—appeal. The sooner her work there was through, the better she would like it.

Because the thought of a pj day with Simon was a twenty on her one-to-ten scale of wanting to do it.

Megan carried a tray holding a plateful of bacon, eggs and biscuits, a glass of orange juice and a mug of coffee into the living room. Simon reclined on the couch and said nothing.

"So, you're still not speaking to me?" she said crisply. "I guess I'll just take this back in the kitchen."

He knew she was unphased by his silent treatment. Probably because of the phone call.

"Wait," he said. The single word stopped her as she started to turn.

The smell of the food drifted to him, making his stomach growl. Megan's replacement had fed him. And she was a good cook. But somehow he felt he hadn't gotten the same nourishment. It was as if he'd missed out on essential vitamins and minerals only Megan could provide. And maybe he'd been wrong yesterday and actually did need his head examined.

"So you *are* speaking to me?" she asked, one eyebrow lifting.

Was he annoyed with her for not being there or himself for noticing it was different without her? Either way, feelings, sensations and sheer sexual awareness dormant for two years were blinking like the warning cockpit lights of the space shuttle with a problem. Because of Megan. He wasn't particularly pleased about it but couldn't seem to find the off switch. Did that matter? Megan was temporary, just until he could hobble on his own two feet. Where was the harm in playing it out?

The harm was he enjoyed himself with her. It felt wrong. It felt wrong to find pleasure in living.

"You abandoned me," he said.

"Oh, puhleeze."

He looked up at her. How did she make shapeless scrubs look so damn good? Her golden hair was parted on the side, then scraped away from her face and held off her neck with a clip. Big blue eyes regarded him with amusement. Before he'd sold his engineering firm, when he'd been actively involved in the business, he'd been able to put fear into people without raising his voice. A single look was enough. But she wasn't intimidated in the least. Admiration for this woman flickered through him. Not for the first time.

"Are you going to torture me with that food? Or bring it over here so I can eat it?"

"I haven't decided yet."

"What do I have to do to help you make up your mind?"

"Stop behaving like a petulant little boy." She stared down at him. "After we talked yesterday, I thought you were okay."

He had been okay, just from the sound of her voice. But that was before he'd learned an important lesson. A day without Megan was like a day without sunshine. It tended to make a man grumpy. When he'd told her the other nurse had finished off what was left of his leg, he'd been joking. But his statement had proven prophetic. The woman could give Hulk Hogan a run for his money. The rest of the day had passed without wit, sarcasm or insult. Boring as hell. Something his life hadn't been since meeting Megan. Something it would be again after she was gone. The fact that he'd noticed the contrast made him uneasy.

"If you're okay, why aren't you talking, Simon?" she prompted.

"I don't have anything to say." At least nothing that he wanted to share.

"So you're ready to lose the attitude?" She shook her head. "You know, I say the same thing to Bayleigh. The statement is usually followed by an order to go to her room until she's pleasant to be around. I could say the same thing to you."

"So what's stopping you?"

If she would go to his room with him, he would be very pleasant to be around. The thought, from out of nowhere, sent a shaft of sexual need straight to his groin. He wanted her and had the painful physical response to prove it.

"That injured leg of yours is stopping me," she said, tilting her head in the general direction of the limb in question. "Your attitude adjustment will just have to take place there on the couch."

"Fair enough," he said. "I'm sorry."

"Wow. You work fast. Okay, then," she said, placing the tray on his thighs.

It barely missed the erect proof that his body was coming back to life even if his spirit never would. Fortunately, she didn't seem to notice the body part in question.

"Are you always so tough?" he asked.

"Always," she said proudly. "It's one of my best qualities."

She turned away and disappeared into the kitchen before he could agree with her. He picked up his fork and made short work of breakfast. Even before finishing his coffee, he felt better—all the requisite vitamins and minerals, he thought, breathing in the fragrance of Megan.

A few minutes later she walked briskly into the room. "It's time for vitals."

He looked down at the empty plate, glass and mug on his tray. "I just did."

"That was vittles, not vitals," she said, laughing. "You know the drill—temperature, pulse, blood pressure."

"They've been normal for five days."

"Doesn't matter. It's all part of the report I give your doctor on your progress. Work with me here, Simon."

"Okay."

"My little lecture was swift and effective." She looked surprised. "Who knew being the mother of a five-year-old would serve me well in nursing a stubborn, disobedient male patient?"

She sat down on the coffee table across from him and did her nurse thing. If any readings were off the scale, she didn't say a word. Just made a notation. After that, it was time to put his injured leg through its paces. She removed the brace.

"Wow, that looks painful." She eyed the bruises that were in a colorful state of healing.

"Yeah," he grunted as she gripped his calf and the sole of his foot and gently pushed it toward his chest. "It is painful, thanks."

She straightened the limb then repeated the movement. "I'm sorry. If you'd take your pain meds—"

"You're not sorry. It gives you great pleasure to torture me."

"Okay. Busted."

She did about ten reps before changing the motion. Then she rotated his foot, gently stretching the muscles in his calf and ankle before going into another exercise. Simon worked out on a regular basis and put himself through the ringer. He was in pretty good shape. But Megan's manipulations made him feel like the very devil. He had a suspicion it had more to do with the touch of her small, strong, healing hands than the contortions of his leg.

Looking at her lovely face made him forget his discomfort.

Before he knew it, she had put the brace in place, then brushed the back of her hand over her forehead. "That's it. Done for today."

"I think I deserve a reward," he said. Her expression of dread told him she was thinking sponge bath. But he had something else in mind.

"What about me? I did all the work. You only sat there."

"You're so right. Yet I feel the need to blow this Popsicle stand."

"What are you talking about?" She brushed a strand of silky gold hair off her forehead.

"I'm feeling cooped up. Let's go to the beach."

"Don't tell me. You want to go surfing," she said. "Shoot the curl. Hang ten. And if your track record is anything to go by—wipe out."

"How did you know?"

Her smile disappeared. "Tell me you're kidding."

"I'm kidding. Gotcha."

"You're going to hell for that, Simon."

Her words held no threat for him. He'd already been there. He could give tours.

She held the TV remote out to him. ''How about a nice, quiet, informative talk show instead?''

He grabbed his crutches and levered himself to a standing position. ''I wasn't kidding about going to the beach.''

''You can't.''

''It's only a block, Megan.''

''I know. But you could fall and do more damage.''

''So you're worried about me?''

''It's my day to watch you, and I don't want anything to happen while you're my responsibility.''

''So come with me. You could probably use some fresh air yourself.''

''I don't want fresh air. I want you to stay here where it's safe.''

Safety was nothing more than an illusion. He wanted fresh air and he would get fresh air—with or without her. Surprisingly, for a man who'd lived a very solitary existence for a very long time, he really wanted it *with* her. And he had one more card to play.

''Suit yourself. I'll go alone.''

He propped the crutches more securely under his arms, gimped to the door and slipped his feet into the deck shoes there. Standing out of the way, he opened it, then glanced over his shoulder. ''Close this after me, would you?'' Without waiting for an answer, he went through the opening.

''Simon—'' She grabbed her sweater from the back of a chair. ''Wait for me.''

A grin turned up the corners of his mouth, but he didn't dare let her see. ''Okay. You can come.''

''You're an evil man,'' she said. But the twinkle in

her eyes gave her away. "If you fall, I'm going to leave you there for seagull bait."

"Deal."

He set the pace and she walked beside him. The day was sunny and clear, with a light, cool breeze. He was wearing a sweatshirt and shorts to accommodate the leg brace, but he wasn't cold. The air felt great after being confined. Megan pulled her sweater tight against the chill as they moved in the shade of the condo building behind his. At the corner, the signal light to cross Pacific Coast Highway was green and they moved to the sidewalk on the other side.

A low cement wall separated the walkway from the sand on the other side. He knew it was as far as he could go. Facing the ocean, he leaned his crutches against the retaining wall and sat down. Megan sat beside him, so close he could almost feel her. So near he didn't have to strain to get a whiff of her unique scent.

"It's beautiful here," she said, taking a deep breath.

"Yeah. So why did I have to bully you into coming down here with me?"

"I didn't think you should or could go this far."

"Oh, ye of little faith."

"Yeah, well, you look like the walking wounded and that doesn't inspire confidence." She took in another deep breath. "My family has a place near the ocean, in Carpinteria."

"I've heard of it. Just south of Santa Barbara. Quaint little beach resort town."

She glanced at him and nodded. "We used to spend summers there. Dad used to join us on weekends and whenever he could get away from work."

"What does he do?"

"He's a doctor. Family practice."

''I guess that's why you went into medicine?''

''Maybe. My sister's a nurse, too.''

''I didn't know you had a sister,'' he said.

''That's because I didn't tell you. I have a brother, too.''

''So tell me about them.''

''Dan is the oldest. He's an architect. Cassie is a little older than me. She lived in Phoenix until recently.''

''What brought her back?''

''A bad relationship there followed by a good job here. She came home unexpectedly and caught her fiancé in bed with her roommate.'' She crossed one shapely leg over the other and braced her hands on the cement wall. Her fingers brushed his thigh, sending sparks of heat arcing through him.

''That's too bad,'' he said automatically.

''Actually, it all worked out for the best. She planned to spend a month at the condo with her friend from school, but Mandy patched things up with her ex-husband, leaving Cass high and dry. As it happens, Kyle Stratton, the son of our duplex neighbors happened to be there, too.''

''Isn't that handy?''

''Fortuitous,'' she said, grinning. ''Cassie's been in love with him since she was a kid. And he finally realized he loves her, too. They're getting married next month.''

''How nice.''

''You don't mean that.''

''Why wouldn't I?'' Who was he to rain on someone else's parade just because it wasn't in the cards for him?

''You don't strike me as the kind of guy who believes in happy endings.''

''Don't let this gruff, battered exterior fool you.''

''Scoff if you want.'' Megan stared at the surf crashing

onto the shore. "I'm glad Cassie found someone. If she can do it, maybe there's hope for me."

"So you're looking for rainbows and moonlight?"

One eyebrow rose. "Who knew a poet lurked beneath that gruff exterior? I don't know. Cassie used to say I was the only one who got dumped worse than she did—"

"What?" he prompted when she stopped suddenly. There was a surprised, almost guilty expression on her face. As if she hadn't meant for that to slip out.

"Nothing. I'm just happy for her." She studied the few people who strolled the sand. "I love the beach. It reminds me of good times when I was a kid. It was a perfect childhood."

"There's no such thing." The words came out harsher than he intended. But when he thought of Marcus, his young life cut short, bitterness, anger and guilt welled up inside him.

"I know," she said, her glance questioning, but she didn't comment on his surly tone. "But mine was just about as good as it gets. I wish—"

"What?"

"Nothing," she said, shaking her head to get loose strands of hair out of her eyes.

"You wish you could give Bayleigh a perfect childhood."

"Yes. How did you know?"

He laughed. "You're an open book, Megan."

"Then you should be able to read my guilt." She sighed. "She's such a good kid."

"Is she actually a kid? She sounded like a miniature adult on the phone."

A smile turned up the corners of her mouth. "We've been working on her technique because she likes answering the phone." She met his gaze, then looked into the distance. "She's so sweet, so uncomplaining. I dream about giving her the kind of growing up experience I had. A home. A family who loves her. A mother and father."

"You need a man."

He hadn't meant to say that. It came out because the longer he was around Megan the more he realized he needed a woman. Forcing himself to ignore the feeling, he tried to concentrate on what she'd said.

"I don't need a man," she huffed.

"I didn't mean it like that. Get your mind out of the gutter, Nurse Brightwell."

"I beg your pardon," she said, self-consciously rubbing a finger along the side of her nose.

"By definition fathers are men. That's all I was saying."

"Can't argue with that logic. The problem is, anyone I'm attracted to isn't willing to take on a child, too. Bayleigh and I are a package deal."

Any man would be lucky to have a woman like Megan in his life. And the blessing of a child... Simon closed his eyes against the soul-deep pain that made it difficult to breathe. He would give anything to have his child back. What kind of guys was she hanging out with who could turn their back on everything she had to offer?

"Apparently, you've been attracted to idiots," he said.

Putting her fists on her hips, she half turned toward him. "I already told you that."

Ah, yes. In the ER when they'd met. He reminded her of the guy who'd walked out on her. That annoyed him.

"Why did you need him?" he asked.

"What? Who?"

"The night of my accident, in the ER. You said he left you when you needed him most. Why did you need him?"

Chapter Eight

Megan's heart stuttered at the question. She couldn't tell Simon that she'd needed Bayleigh's father for emotional support because their child was going blind. The only man who could possibly care about their little girl in the same way she did had the spine of a slug. He hadn't loved her and he'd slithered away because he couldn't face the problems and difficulties of raising an imperfect, sightless child.

If she told Simon any of that, it would lead to more questions she wasn't prepared to answer. And he was in no condition to hear the responses.

She glanced at him. They were sitting side by side on the cement retaining wall, positioned as if it were an old-fashioned love seat. Her feet were in the sand. He was angled the other way, his long legs stretched out on the sidewalk paralleling the street. They were close enough that if either of them shifted, their shoulders brushed. His was solid and strong, a fact she should ignore, or at least pretend to. She was his nurse. Any attraction she felt was inappropriate and unprofessional.

She stole a look at him. The breeze blew his slightly too long dark hair off his forehead and the sunlight revealed in colorful detail his scabbed-over scrapes and fading bruises. But it was his eyes that drew her attention.

Genuine interest glittered in his gaze, making him look far different from when she'd first met him. That night his eyes had been dull, flat—lifeless. Today, with the sound of the surf crashing nearby, sunshine and blue sky overhead, he was showing signs of caring—dare she say it—about life.

She shook her head. The time was coming when she would let him know what a difference his sacrifice had made. She hoped between now and then the right words would come to her to ease his loss and let him know how grateful she was for Bayleigh's gift of sight. But today wasn't the day.

She wouldn't tell him her daughter could see because his son had died.

"Megan?"

She met his quizzical gaze. "Hmm?"

"I wasn't talking nuclear physics. It didn't seem like that hard a question."

"I'm sorry. What did you ask?"

"Why did you need Bayleigh's father?"

"You know, I don't think answering personal questions is part of my job." It was all she could think of to try and deflect the question. But she had a feeling Simon wouldn't let her get away with it that easily.

"Oh, really?" He crossed his arms over his chest and tucked his fingertips into his armpits.

Why couldn't he ever disappoint her? "Yeah. I'm here

to make sure you get better. Telling you about my personal life isn't part of my job description.''

''So what we have here is a double standard. You get to grill me like a raw hamburger, but I don't get to ask questions about you?''

''In a word?'' She met his gaze. ''Yes.''

He shook his head. ''I don't think so. You can't tell me when you're on assignment you don't talk to your patients about yourself. And I mean personal stuff.''

''Why would I?''

''Because it's what women do. To bond.''

''How do you know that?''

''I watch daytime talk shows.'' One corner of his mouth lifted. ''Or maybe I heard it from my mother-in-law, I mean *ex* mother-in-law.''

Megan couldn't let on that she knew Janet. Another subject that would lead to questions she couldn't answer. Oh, what a tangled web we weave—and all that, she thought. ''Women do share details of their lives. But you're not a woman and I'm not trying to bond with you.''

''Okay. It took threats to get you to walk with me to the beach. If that's what it takes to get an answer to my question, I'm not above threatening.''

She knew he would come up with something medically unsound. ''Like I said before, you're an evil man.''

''You have no idea. Now. Why did the guy walk out when you needed him?''

''Isn't it obvious?'' She had no alternative but to answer his question. But she didn't have to tell him everything. ''I had his child.''

She sighed, uncomfortable with keeping the details from him. The fact that it was only half a lie didn't help much.

He shifted his position on the wall, then shoved his fingers through his hair. ''You said when you needed him *most* he walked out. That implies something out of the ordinary was going on. What was it, Megan?''

She stiffened at his words. For goodness' sake, he'd briefly lost consciousness the night of his accident. Why couldn't he have forgotten that one, small, four-letter qualifier? It made all the difference.

''What was going on out of the ordinary?'' She looked heavenward as she thought about how to answer. ''Bayleigh was the first child for both of us, so we were in unfamiliar territory. There were the two-o'clock feedings that didn't necessarily occur at two o'clock on the dot, but any time of the night she decided she was hungry. Then there was the incessant crying you could set your watch by at our dinner time. Toss into that mix diaper changing and you've got a life-altering experience he couldn't handle at the time I most needed support.''

''So he couldn't deal with being a father?''

''That's about the size of it,'' she agreed. And he didn't love them enough to try.

''He was a jerk.''

''Yeah,'' she said. ''Big jerk.''

''But not all men are.''

''You couldn't prove that by me. I've dated some. Either all of you are idiots, or I'm a just a jerk magnet. You can't pick up a magazine without seeing an article about nice single guys looking for a good woman to settle down with. But I can't seem to find one.''

''There's another possibility.''

''And what would that be?'' She pushed a strand of hair from her eyes, then tucked it behind her ear.

''Maybe you're subconsciously attracted to the wrong men.''

"Excuse me?" She turned in his direction, bending her knee to rest her thigh on the wall so she could sit facing him. Now he had her full attention.

"Has it occurred to you that you deliberately pick men who aren't interested in a ready-made family? A package deal?"

"About that daytime TV you've been watching? Have you by any chance been tuned in to Dr. Phil? The guru of 'your life is empty because you *want* it to be empty'?"

One corner of his mouth turned up. "Your life isn't empty. You just don't have a man in it. And you don't because you're afraid to trust."

"So, Dr. Reynolds. What do you suggest I do about the situation?"

"Simon says get over it."

He shrugged, again drawing her attention to his broad shoulders and wide chest. His navy sweatshirt with the U.C.L.A. logo on the front hid the delicious details from view. But he'd been practically naked since she'd met him and the thought sent heat pouring through her. She was acutely attracted to him. Once the truth, the whole truth and nothing but the truth was out, he was the last man who would be interested in her and Bayleigh as a package deal. That was irrefutable proof that there could be truth to his theory.

"People spend gazillions of dollars on therapy every year," she said, shaking her head. "And all they have to do is just get over it?"

"Why not? When the horse throws you, get right back in the saddle."

"If it's that simple, Simon, how come you haven't taken your own advice?"

When the words came pouring out, she wanted them back in the worst way. Or she wanted to kick herself.

Apparently, there was a short in the wiring from her brain to her mouth. When the shadows crossed his face, she started to touch him, to apologize. Then she remembered. She wasn't supposed to know his story. All he'd told her was that his wife had divorced him because he was a workaholic. The response she'd just snapped out to his advice was what the average person would say. So she forced herself to wait for him to answer.

"You mean why am I alone?" He ran his fingers through his hair and stared at the multistory condominium building across the street. Then he met her gaze. "I don't want to get back in the saddle."

"So you're a do-as-I-say-not-as-I-do kind of guy?"

"I suppose."

"Maybe I don't want to get back in the saddle, either," she said. "Why is that any different from you?"

"I'm not the one who wants to give my daughter a certain kind of childhood."

The bleak expression on his face tore at her heart. Whoever had coined the phrase "no pain, no gain" should be shot. He needed to talk about Marcus and, when he did, she knew it was going to hurt—badly. Damn, she hated this. If she didn't owe this man more than she could ever repay, she'd have walked away right then and there. But she had to hide her reaction, because she wasn't supposed to know.

He didn't respond to pity. Somehow she had to muster some backbone or he would be suspicious.

She swung both legs over the wall and stood in front of him on the sidewalk. Looking down at him, she said, "Simon, I don't know if you were any good at engineering. But I can tell you one thing."

"What's that?" he asked, interest gathering in his eyes.

"Don't even try to give Dr. Phil a run for his money. In case you were considering it, I recommend keeping your day job."

He stood, balancing carefully on both feet as he grabbed his crutches and tucked them beneath his armpits. "Don't shoot the messenger, Megan, just because you don't like the message."

"Is that what I was doing?" She walked over to the signal and pushed the walk button.

"Yes. And for the record, I don't have a day job to keep."

"Why is that?"

"Because I sold my company after—"

After Marcus died. She knew. But she had to get him to volunteer it. "After what?" she prompted.

"The divorce," he said. "They—the corporation who bought me out—wanted me to do some consulting. But I—"

"What?"

"Didn't want to," he finished.

So they were at an impasse. When the signal changed, they moved slowly across the street. Megan glanced at the brooding look on his face. Unfortunately, life was a series of traumas punctuated by having to do things you didn't want to.

She didn't want the burden of knowing Simon's secret. She didn't want to be his nurse. She especially wished this attraction to him would disappear. If only she didn't enjoy talking to him, joking with him and being with him. And if he wasn't quite so easy on the eyes, her job would be a walk in the park.

She wondered what she'd ever done to deserve this punishment. Because her assignment wasn't even half-over.

* * *

Simon hadn't been able to get Megan off his mind. It had been two days since they'd talked on the beach, a week since his accident. They'd fallen into a pattern. Her ten-hour shift began promptly at seven in the morning. After taking his vitals she made vittles. He smiled at the memory that had become a running joke. He ate breakfast and, after straightening the kitchen, she put his leg through the painful paces that were beginning to show results. Then came his favorite part—the bath.

But now she gathered supplies and made him wash all over by himself. He wondered what she'd say if he told her he could move around pretty well. If she knew he wasn't letting on about his progress, she'd probably quit again. And this time he had a feeling she wouldn't come back.

But every evening when she fixed dinner for him, he knew it was almost time for her to leave. She insisted on spending the evening with her daughter. He wanted to ask her to stay, so he wouldn't have to eat alone. He didn't. He let her go without a word, then he counted the minutes and hours until she came back. Until he could bask in her sunshine for a while longer.

She was committed to another week of nursing him. Only seven days. Then she would be gone for good. It was something he didn't want to think about.

Today she was in the kitchen cooking breakfast. The smell of bacon drifted to him, making his mouth water. Almost as much as the sight of Megan Brightwell in her work clothes, which looked like pajamas. What would she say to a pj day? With him?

''Simon, do you want orange juice?'' She appeared in the kitchen doorway.

From his usual place on the couch in the living room,

he watched her wipe her hands on a dish towel. ''Just coffee.''

Her hands stilled. ''You need the vitamin C. It promotes healing.''

''If you're going to boss me into drinking it anyway, why did you ask if I wanted some?''

''Just trying to be polite.'' She grinned, then she was gone.

She was like a strobe light—all brightness and energy. A welcome distraction.

Simon hadn't thought about anyone but himself for a long time—pathetic but true. Until Megan. She walked into his life with spunk and spice and everything nice. But that wasn't the only reason he couldn't get her off his mind.

Ever since the other day when she'd talked about Bayleigh's father walking out and why, he couldn't forget the way she'd looked. He'd watched the tension in her face, the pain in her eyes. Didn't they say the eyes were the window to the soul? If that was true, Megan's soul needed therapy as much as his leg.

And he couldn't shake the feeling that she was holding something back. He'd never been especially intuitive. If he had, he'd have known how unhappy Donna was long before she'd announced she was leaving him. But it was different with Megan. He would swear she had something to tell him. It was as if, in some weird way, his pain was connected to hers, giving him insight via some invisible conduit. How crazy was he?

She was right. He shouldn't give Dr. Phil a run for his money. He was a fool to think about Megan. But he couldn't help it.

She walked out of the kitchen carrying a tray. He could

see steam rising from the plate and the mug of coffee beside it. Then there was that tall glass of juice.

''Here you go.'' She bent and set the tray on his lap.

The fragrance of flowers that surrounded her mixed with the smell of cooked bacon and eggs. Her cheeks were pink from the heat of standing over a hot frying pan. Or at least he thought so until her gaze didn't quite meet his.

''So vitamin C promotes healing,'' he said, taking a long drink of juice.

''That's what I hear.'' She walked into the kitchen and came back with a mug of coffee. Then she sat in one of the wing chairs. It was her habit to keep him company while he ate. She always had breakfast with her daughter.

''You don't think I'm progressing fast enough so you're bringing in the big guns?''

''I'm merely attempting to provide well-balanced meals.''

''To promote healing.''

''Of course.''

''So you can go on to your next assignment. Someone who isn't saturated fat?'' He thought that was as good a time as any to eat a piece of bacon.

As she blew on her coffee, her gaze—tinged with guilt—met his over the rim of the cup. ''Simon, you're progressing extremely well. Very soon you won't need me.''

''But not today.''

''Not today,'' she agreed. ''It's been a week and you need those stitches out. You'll want to see the doctor—''

''Why?'' He forked up some scrambled eggs as he watched her.

''The wound should be looked at to make sure it's healed sufficiently. Checked for infection.''

"You can do that."

"I'm not a doctor."

"It doesn't take twelve years of medical school to see it's healed, then snip and pluck."

He ate a piece of toast—wheat he noticed—and watched emotions drift across her face like clouds floating over the sun. Reluctance, dread, anticipation, fear. But she didn't say anything.

"Come on, Megan. I've taken my own stitches out before and lived to tell about it."

"So do it."

He rolled his shoulder, testing the level of discomfort. "It's hard to reach. And I can't do it one-handed."

"Okay." She met his gaze. "But sooner or later you're going to have to see the doctor about that leg."

"Okay, I will," he agreed.

"You're lying, aren't you?"

He grinned. "Yeah."

Without comment, she crossed one slender leg over the other and sipped her coffee. The silence stretched between them as he finished his breakfast and put down his fork. She rose and put her mug on the tray, then lifted it from his lap and started for the kitchen.

"Wait a minute," he said.

"What's wrong?"

"The least you could do is argue with me. Don't you care what happens to my leg?"

One corner of her full mouth quirked up. "Of course." She started to turn away.

"If you're concerned, why didn't you try harder to convince me to let the doc have a look?"

She smiled at him—a serene, indulgent sort of look. "Simon, Simon, Simon. As a rule, a man's a fool. When it's hot he wants it cool. When it's cool he wants it hot. Always wanting what is not."

"What's that supposed to mean?"

"It means you're acting like a cross little boy who's not getting his way. I can't make you do anything. I'm not going to waste my breath arguing with you for your entertainment." Then she turned away.

He grinned at her back as she walked the tray into the kitchen. She sure had his number. And, damn, it felt good to smile—a genuine, spontaneous one that split his face from ear to ear.

A few minutes later she came back and stood beside him. "Okay, let me take a look at those stitches. Take your shirt off."

"Right." He grabbed the hem of his black T-shirt and yanked it up and over his head.

She sat beside him on the couch. Her medical bag was on the coffee table next to his propped-up leg and she leaned over to take scissors and tweezer-looking things from it. As she did, her cotton top pulled snugly along the slender line of her back. Not an especially sexy move, but it worked for him. His palm itched to touch her, rub his hand up and down, feel her heat through the material of her scrub top.

She straightened and met his gaze, then her own skittered away. The pulse at the base of her throat fluttered. He wasn't a health-care professional, but he would swear it was a shade too fast. Did he make her nervous? The thought pleased him in a blatantly male, self-satisfied way.

"Now, then," she said. "This won't hurt."

"So I can leave my biting stick in the drawer?"

"Very funny. I think you can handle this. But the stitches could stick, so you might feel a pull."

Apparently, she wasn't content with her angle of attack, because she stood, then bent her knee and knelt on the sofa. She peeled away the tape and lifted the nonstick square covering the area. He watched her small, sure hands as she quickly snipped the sutures, then efficiently plucked them out. He hardly felt a thing. In his shoulder.

Other areas were definitely pulling tight. He wasn't sure if it was her zinger about him acting like a cross little boy, but he felt the need to know if he was right that she noticed him as a man.

When she finished with his shoulder, she looked at him and said, "I think you're going to live."

"Yeah?" He curved his arm around her waist and tugged her down, onto his lap.

"Simon, what—"

He cupped her cheek in his hand and watched awareness chase the surprised expression from her blue eyes. He was going to kiss her and she knew it. He meant business and he was going to do a thorough job. The pounding pulse at the base of her throat told him she knew that, too. Finally, when she didn't move, he lowered his head and touched her lips with his own.

Slanting his mouth over hers, he moved slowly and deliberately. He traced the seam of her lips with his tongue and she instantly opened for him. When he dipped inside the honeyed interior, the sweetness of her drove him to the edge. It had been so long since he'd touched a woman like this, since he'd even wanted to. But there was something about Megan he couldn't ignore. She gave as good as she got, so vital, so alive.

She made him want more; she made him want—period.

He dragged his mouth from hers and trailed kisses across her cheek and down to her throat. His breathing was ragged; he could barely draw air into his lungs. It was as if she'd knocked the wind out of him. But he could no more pull away from her than he could change the past.

Her hand caressed his bare chest until she slid it up to his neck. In its wake, her palm left a trail of fire. He moved his hand from her face down her shoulder and rested it at her waist. After denying himself for so long, the need to touch her bare skin, to explore the texture of her silky flesh, was a temptation he couldn't resist.

He found the hem of her shirt and nudged his fingertips beneath, sliding upward. Over her flat midriff, he explored. He savored the softness, the warmth, and settled his palm over her bra. Only thin, nearly transparent lace was between his hand and her small, perfect breast. He heard her sharp intake of breath when he took her nipple between his thumb and forefinger, feeling it grow hard.

His insides were like dry tinder. Her moan of pleasure was like a tossed match. Heat exploded inside him. His heart thundered. Where was the heart monitor when you really needed it?

"As a rule a man's a fool," he said, his voice husky.

"When it's hot he wants it cool," she whispered.

"Not this time."

He was hard and his erection pressed against the softness of her hip as she burrowed into his chest. She slid her hand from his neck and over his shoulder, fast, frantic movements as if she couldn't touch him enough. He felt her brush the spot where she'd just removed his stitches. He felt no pain, made no sound, but she froze. In the next instant, she sat up out of his arms, then wiggled off his lap.

"This is wrong," she said, breathing hard as she looked down at him. "It's inappropriate."

"It felt pretty damned appropriate to me. How is it wrong?"

"Let me count the ways," she said. "I'm your nurse. I kissed you. That behavior crosses the line between personal and professional. I could lose my job."

"First of all, I started it. Second, no one will find out because I don't plan to tell. Do you?"

"Of course not." She put her hands on her hips as her chest rose and fell rapidly. "This can't happen again, Simon. Not ever."

"Megan, I—"

"I mean it. I need you to promise or I won't be back. You can call and have them send someone else."

He didn't want anyone else. He also knew she meant what she said. "Okay."

"Okay. Good." She let out a long breath. "Now I need to clean up the kitchen."

He didn't say anything, just watched her walk away. And tried to ignore the painful throbbing in his groin. It was hard evidence that he wanted her. And she was right about him being a rule-breaker, because he hadn't promised not to kiss her again. All he'd said was "okay."

After two years, Simon felt alive again. He had Megan to thank—or to blame. He wasn't sure which. Nor was he particularly happy about not wanting to let her go.

But none of that changed the fact that he was coming back to life and he didn't know how to make it stop.

Chapter Nine

"Your pocket is ringing," Simon said.

Megan looked at him sitting on the couch with his splinted leg elevated and an open book on his lap. She was still mad at him for that kiss two days ago. Or at least trying to be.

"Thanks. If you hadn't pointed it out, I never would have heard that noise loud enough to wake the deaf."

It wasn't easy to stay angry when he looked so good—handsome as opposed to innocent. There was nothing remotely angelic about the dark-blue T-shirt clinging to the muscular contour of his broad chest and pulling snugly around his upper arms. She'd bullied him into letting her trim his hair and she hadn't done a half-bad job, but she kind of missed the rebellious, longish hair brushing the neck of his shirt. It was almost time for her to leave for the day and she was making sure everything he needed was easily accessible to him.

But as he regarded her, his blue eyes simmering with a hint of humor, she struggled to resist smiling. She was still mad at him. At least she was doing her darnedest to be. It was her best defense against the mysterious thing that drew her to him. What was it? Could she put up a better resistance if she named it?

She wouldn't call him especially charming. Definitely not charming, she thought, looking at the dark, intense expression on his face.

Still, humor was shining through more often these days. Then there was his in-your-face masculinity and the come-hither expression in his eyes that turned her insides to quivering gelatin. He was probably the sexiest man she'd ever met. And so much more. It was hard not to care about someone who cared so deeply he still grieved.

Putting her back to him, she pulled the cell phone from her pocket. "Hello?"

"Hi, Mommy. What took you so long to answer the phone?"

"Hi, sweetie. It wasn't long, was it?" Had she zoned in on Simon so completely she'd lost track of time? This was where she changed the subject. "Is everything okay? I'll be at Grammy's in a little while to pick you up."

"I'm fine. But I want to stay with Grammy."

"What's going on?"

It was Friday and her mother had picked the child up from school and would keep her until Megan could get there after work. With her cell phone to her ear and Simon close enough to hear every word, she listened to her daughter.

"I want to have a sleepover. Grammy and Grampy are having chicken nuggets and French fries for dinner. You know that's their favorite."

"And I guess you don't like chicken nuggets and fries

anymore,'' she said, making her voice completely serious as she grinned. Her daughter would eat that seven nights a week if no one forced on her a well-rounded diet.

''They're okay,'' the little girl answered.

Megan could tell she was trying not to sound excited. ''I don't mind if you have dinner there. But I don't know about a sleepover, sweetie.''

''But Mo-om, we're going to watch a video. And play games. Grammy's going to let me do stuff on her computer. And Grampy's going to get powdered sugar donuts for breakfast.'' She stopped, obviously listening to someone in the background. ''Grammy says I have to have an apple slice for every donut. And milk. It's not a school night,'' she finished, her voice just this side of a whine.

Megan smiled. ''Can you put Grammy on the phone?''

''Okay. Grammy?''

The shout came over so loud and clear, Megan held the phone away from her ear. Then she heard her mother's voice. ''Megan?''

''Hi, Mom. Are you sure this sleepover is okay? She's pretty high energy. She'll wear you and Dad out.''

''She's no trouble. We love having her. You know that. And she loves being here.''

''What's not to like? You guys spoil her rotten. She gets to do everything she wants. Her every whim is indulged. Why would she give you trouble?''

Her mother laughed. ''Are we that bad? Don't answer that,'' she added quickly. ''It's a grandmother's prerogative to spoil. I did my time with you and Dan and Cassie. My only obligation with Bayleigh is to keep her safe and happy while she's with me. Don't scold me, Megan. I earned it.''

Megan shook her head and laughed. ''When you put it like that, how can I say no?''

"Good. Mommy said okay," she told Bayleigh, who was no doubt standing at her elbow. A resounding cheer came through loud and clear. "Besides, Megan, you're working so hard. It will give you a chance to take it easy for one evening. I get the feeling this particular nursing assignment is pretty demanding."

Megan glanced at Simon, who was watching her. The smoldering look in his eyes sent sparks dancing over her skin. Definitely demanding. But after the kiss she couldn't forget, she didn't want to think about *what* he was demanding. The other day, if she hadn't already removed his sutures, the heat the two of them generated would have melted them. Ever since, she'd had a heck of a time keeping her mind on good medicine instead of, good God, why doesn't he do that again. For one thing, she'd made him promise not to.

If her mother only knew the half of it, how intense this assignment was. Megan had only told her it would last two weeks without a replacement, as requested by the patient. Her parents didn't know that she was caring for the man whose son had donated corneas to Bayleigh.

"Megan?"

"I'm here. Tell Daddy hi. Don't let Bayleigh run him ragged."

"I won't. She wants to say goodbye."

"Okay. Bye, Mom. And thanks. Love you." She waited several seconds.

"Mommy? I love you. Bye."

"Wait. I love you, too. Be good for Grammy and Grampy."

"I will. Love you. Bye."

Then the phone went silent. Megan closed it up and slid it into her pocket. She braced herself, then turned to look at Simon. "I guess I'll get your dinner started."

"I couldn't help overhearing that your responsibilities for the evening end when you're finished with me."

She nodded. "Bayleigh's spending the night with my folks."

His laserlike gaze locked on her. "Is that a problem?"

He must have heard the what-am-I-going-to-do-with-myself tone in her voice. She was so accustomed to responsibility, without any she felt like a boat ripped from its moorings.

"Not a problem, except for the attitude she'll bring home with her. But after I get you squared away for the night, I'm footloose and fancy-free."

"Then don't go."

"What?"

"Why don't you stay and have dinner with me? I can't promise much but I guarantee it won't be chicken nuggets and fries."

It was a really bad idea. She knew because of how badly she wanted to say yes. Because of the way her heart lurched and the way her blood sang through her veins, bringing a heated flush to her skin.

"Thanks, Simon. But I really have to go home."

"Why? Your daughter is with her grandparents. What's so pressing?"

"Would you believe a pair of slippers, an easy chair and a good book?"

"I can do better than that."

His deep, husky tone invaded her body, acting on her senses like warm brandy, caressing her from the inside out. She'd just bet he could do better. A pair of hands that would make her an easy mark and a good kiss that could so easily lead her down the primrose path to paradise followed by pain.

"Simon, you don't have to entertain me. I really just need to get home."

"What are you afraid of, Megan?"

"Nothing. I—"

"I know you're off the clock and my welfare is not your duty, but it would do me good to have your company tonight."

She met his gaze. Emotions swirled in his eyes as a muscle worked in his jaw. The admission had come with a price, and it wasn't cheap.

"Why?" she asked. It seemed he'd opened the door a crack and maybe she could get him to swing it wider.

He looked down for several moments, then said, "I don't want to eat alone. Again. Every night you leave something to nuke or feed me before you go. I can't remember the last time I had dinner with a beautiful woman."

He thought she was beautiful? "Now I know you're not serious."

"You'd be wrong. And it's about time you took the night off from cooking."

"Don't tell me. You're going to do the honors?"

"Sure." One dark eyebrow rose in challenge.

She put her hands on her hips and stared down at him. "You don't have two good legs to stand on."

"One is a hundred percent, and I've progressed to needing only a single crutch for the other. But me cooking is not what I had in mind. There's an Italian place close by that delivers. Let me show my appreciation. It's the least I can do to thank you for—everything."

He thought she was beautiful? She couldn't seem to get her brain to record over those words. Her insides went all warm and gooey, like sweet, melted chocolate. *Blow in my ear and I'll follow you anywhere,* she thought.

Danger, Megan Brightwell. The message came through loud and clear. She should say thanks, but no thanks.

"Simon, you don't have to thank me. It's my job."

"Okay. But in a few minutes it won't be. How often do you get pampered? Let me take you out to dinner—so to speak." He smiled, a devastating flash of white teeth that was too appealing for words and had her heart doing the happy dance.

And he was finally reaching out.

Damn. Why did she have to think about that?

For the first time, he was telling her how he felt and what he needed. It was another sign that he was opening up. Maybe he was ready. Maybe it was time she helped him begin to deal with the tragedy of losing his son so he could move forward with his life. How could she walk away now? It's what she'd been waiting and hoping for.

She looked at him. "It's an offer I'm finding very hard to refuse."

"Good, then—"

She held up her hand. "I haven't officially accepted. Ground rules first."

He folded his arms over his broad chest. "And they are?"

"Actually it's only one," she said, swallowing hard. If she'd ever seen a more masculine sight than Simon Reynolds, all shoulders and bulging biceps, she couldn't recall. "No more kissing. If you do, I'll have to quit before the assignment ends."

"We've been over this before. So, okay," he agreed with a casual shrug of those terrific shoulders.

That was too easy. There was a loophole somewhere that she just wasn't seeing, but that didn't really matter.

She was going to stay. She had to. What if he never reached out again?

"Thank you, Simon. I'd love to have dinner with you."

Two hours later, Megan was glad she'd stayed. Simon had phoned Marchetti's, the Italian restaurant he'd told her about, and ordered the Takeout for Two special. He'd had the strangest expression on his face when suggesting angel-hair pasta with herbs and sun-dried tomatoes along with a lovely Caesar salad. She'd had no objection. The package included a bottle of the house wine—a wonderful cabernet-merlot combination that was nearly as smooth as Simon's voice when he'd said she was beautiful—in that roundabout way.

In addition to plastic utensils, sturdy paper plates and disposable place mats, the distinctive takeout included complimentary plastic wineglasses with everything featuring Marchetti's logo. The crowning touch was two red candles and holders that the delivery guy, acting as a waiter, had lit after arranging everything on the dining room table.

He'd turned out the kitchen lights, lit the gas log in the fireplace, then dimmed the chandelier above the table, setting the mood he assumed a man ordering Takeout for Two would want. Any second she expected the complimentary violinist to stroll in and start playing. After payment that included a generous tip from Simon, Marchetti's best departed with a wide smile and a reminder to keep them in mind for their next romantic occasion.

Yeah, like that was going to happen. But it didn't mean Megan couldn't enjoy the moment. Bayleigh was safe and happy with her grandparents. So Megan was off the clock, personally and professionally.

Simon sat across from her at the table with his leg

propped up on the chair beside him. His single crutch rested nearby.

He held up his wine. ''Here's to—''

''A carefree dinner,'' she finished.

''Whatever you say.'' He sipped, then set down his wine, trading it for his fork.

She drank and the liquid slid down her throat easily. Before she knew it, her glass was empty. She watched Simon pick up the bottle and refill it. Candlelight flickered over the angles of his face, giving him a brooding, mysterious look that worked for her way too well. She was warm inside and out and was pretty sure it was the man not the wine. The depth of feeling she experienced for the amount of time she'd known him scared her. But there wasn't a problem as long as she kept everything under control.

''This is lovely, Simon. Thank you.''

''The pleasure is all mine.'' There was an intense expression in his eyes as he looked at her. Five-o'clock shadow darkening his jaw gave him a dangerously sexy air. ''I wonder if Bayleigh knows how lucky she is.''

''Of course she does. Right now she's stuffed full of nuggets, fries and whatever else her heart desires.''

''That's not what I meant. Every night she has you across the table from her.''

The words coated her bruised soul like honey and lemon soothing a raw throat. Simon wasn't the only one living in isolation. How long had it been since she'd had dinner alone with a handsome man? A sexy man? A man who tempted her with a single look? She couldn't remember. She tried to tell herself that it didn't matter—Bayleigh was all the family she needed.

But at a moment like this, Megan couldn't deny she was lonely. Because she was a woman with a child, her dating pool was dry. Either men shied away from the added responsibility and complication or they were lousy father material.

Always the thought was there that her daughter deserved more. A complete, two-parent home like she'd had was her dream for Bay. A dad who would love her. But the prospects of that actually happening weren't looking too good.

What did look good was Simon opening up. Megan took it as a very positive sign that he'd brought up Bayleigh.

"So tell me about her father." His gaze rested on her face, and he seemed to be studying her.

Megan nearly choked on her pasta. "I'd rather not."

"Why?"

"It would spoil my appetite or interfere with my digestion. Or both."

One corner of his mouth quirked up. "How did you meet him?"

She considered not answering, but she'd learned one thing about Simon: when he wanted something, he didn't let it drop.

"He's a drug rep for a pharmaceutical company. The hospital where I was doing my clinical training was his territory. We met in the cafeteria."

"How long did you go out with him?"

"Until he disappeared."

His eyes hardened. "Did your parents like him?"

"You mean did they have any idea he was a spineless weasel?"

"Yeah." He twirled a forkful of pasta and put it in his mouth.

"They were okay with him right up until I found out I was pregnant and he didn't propose marriage."

''Why didn't he?''

She shrugged as she chewed her salad. It didn't take a rocket scientist to answer the question; an engineer like Simon wouldn't have too much trouble figuring it out. ''Isn't it obvious?''

''Not to me.''

''You're a guy, Simon. What do you think?''

''I think I want you to tell me. He didn't ask you to marry him. But he didn't walk out on you then.''

''How do you know?''

''Because you said he walked out when you needed him most. I assumed that was when you told him you were pregnant. But after what you said the other day it was clear he hung in. At first.''

She met his gaze across the candlelit table. Simon was asking why she hadn't married her daughter's father. What he really wanted to know was what happened to make him walk out. It was the only thing she couldn't reveal.

''He didn't love me. Or his child. There. I said it. Are you happy now?''

''No. A man doesn't walk out on his child. Clearly, he's pond scum.''

She nodded. ''I couldn't agree more. Now can we change the subject? How about those Lakers? Lovely weather we're having. Do you think the Democrats will win back the White House?''

''Does she ever ask about him?''

''Who?'' Megan knew good and well who. But what had happened to getting him to open up? He'd gone on the offensive like a wide receiver with a Hail Mary pass and she couldn't seem to strip the ball out of his hands. This was supposed to be all about him sharing with her. She was losing her grip on the situation.

"Come on, Megan. You know who. Does Bayleigh ever ask about her father? Why she doesn't see him?"

"That's not something I want to talk about."

"You know when two people are friends—"

"Is that what we are?" she asked.

"I like to think so. I respect you and your profession. You boss me around." He shrugged. "It works. A match made in heaven. But there's a definite lack of cooperation on your part—in the information-sharing department."

"Just because we've spent a lot of time together, doesn't mean I have to tell you the personal details of my life."

"I'm not asking about personal stuff. I was wondering about Bayleigh."

"She is personal. And doing just fine, thank you for asking."

He leaned back in his chair and stared at her as a muscle worked in his jaw. "That's it?"

"I don't owe you anything, Simon."

"Maybe not. But you pried information out of me like a dentist working on an impacted wisdom tooth."

She laughed. "You call what you told me information? Three—no three and a half details." She held up the appropriate number of fingers. "You're divorced. Because you're a workaholic. And you don't have a job."

"What's the half?"

"You sold your company—that not having a job thing is sort of a by-product." As she'd ticked off everything he'd told her, one by one she'd curled her fingers into a fist. "A lot of men are divorced workaholics, but they don't sell the company. They don't toss the baby out with the bathwater. What's your story?"

"I don't have one. Like you, everything's fine."

"Liar. Something's eating at you. Three trips to the

ER in less than two years because of your dangerous hobbies? The things you said the night they brought you in gave me the impression you were almost sorry about surviving. You've quit more than your job, Simon. Most people don't give up that easily. Most people try to hang on to their company. Most people—''

He stood up so fast, his chair scooted back and tilted, almost toppling against the wall. ''What the hell do you know about it? I'm not like most people.''

''Why?'' she asked, standing, too.

His eyes were blazing. He slapped his palms on the table as he leaned forward and glared. ''Most men don't lose their ex-wife and son in a car accident.''

Megan blinked. She felt like the defense attorney who'd just hammered away at the prosecution's star witness and come up with the piece of information necessary to clear her client. She could hardly believe she'd gotten what she'd wanted. ''What did you say?''

Without his crutch, he limped into the living room and sank down onto the couch. He ran the fingers of both hands through his hair, then rubbed a hand across his neck.

She sat down beside him, so close that their thighs brushed. She put her hand on his forearm and felt the warm skin. ''Simon?''

He glanced at her, then away and out the window. ''They died, Megan. Both of them.''

''I see.''

He laughed, and there was anything but humor in the sound. It was tinged with bitter self-loathing. ''You don't see anything.''

''Were you driving?'' she asked. Her stomach dropped to her toes at the idea.

He shook his head. ''Marcus was supposed to be with

me that weekend. Donna and I shared joint custody after the divorce. We worked out a schedule. You know how it is. Every other holiday, every other summer, every other weekend. It was my every other."

"What happened?" she asked, willing him to get it all out. So afraid he would shut her out before he did.

"I had a business trip overseas." He glanced at her, his eyes brimming with deep, profound pain. "Marcus was upset because I'd promised to take him to a hockey game that weekend. I told him there would be other games—" He stopped when his voice caught. His shoulders hunched as he hung his head. "I never saw him alive again. He was gone before I could get back."

She squeezed his arm. "And you're playing 'what if.' It's a game you can't win, Simon."

"No?" When he met her gaze, his look held harsh irony. "If I'd taken him like I should have, he would be alive. If business hadn't come first. If he'd been with me as arranged. If he hadn't been with his mom. If we'd gone to the game, he would still be here."

And if Marcus hadn't died, Bayleigh might not be able to see. To learn to write her name in kindergarten. To pick out her favorite purple dress and the matching lavender top. Oh, God, this was breaking her heart.

She took his big hand between both of hers. "Listen to me, Simon. Please." There was no reaction. "Can you hear me?" His only response was a nod. "Stop it right now. If you keep doing this you'll go crazy. No one knows why these things happen. Fate. Karma. Destiny. Did you know Donna was going to have a fatal accident?"

"No." The word was harsh, grating, like gravel on concrete.

"If you had known, would you have gone on that business trip? If you'd known keeping Marcus with you as arranged would save his life, would you have canceled your travel plans?''

''In a heartbeat,'' he breathed.

''Wouldn't life be simple if we could see the future? If I'd known my daughter's father would bail on me, would I have gone out with him in the first place? Of course not.''

''But you said something positive came out of it. He gave you your daughter. My son is gone. There's nothing good about that.''

She could help him make sense of the loss if he would let her. But he wasn't ready to hear it yet.

Megan willed herself to patience as she rested her chin on his shoulder. ''We can't know the future, Simon. All we can do is put one foot in front of the other day after day. We do the best we can, make the best decisions we're capable of making with the information we've got. You loved him. His mother loved him. You had no reason to believe your son wouldn't be safe with her.''

He pressed the heels of his palms against his eyes. ''I miss him so much it hurts.'' His tone was tortured.

Megan ached for him and played her own game of ''if only.'' If only there was a surgical procedure, an injection, some medical therapy that would take away his pain. But all he had was her. She'd pushed until he'd let her in, and she prayed now for the words to keep him from closing up again. She'd never felt more inadequate in her life.

''Simon, listen to me. I won't say that I have any idea what you're feeling. I don't even want to imagine what it would feel like to lose my child. And I don't know what I would do in your shoes—''

He looked at her then, his eyes blazing as hot as the

flames crackling in the fireplace. "Don't you dare say you're sorry. I swear I'll go in-line skating on crutches."

"Even if I'd been planning to say it, wild horses couldn't drag the words out of me now." She didn't know where she found the courage to go on, but she did because the words had to be said. "Simon, I want you to want to live again—"

Her voice broke. The lump lodged in her throat made it impossible to speak. Tears burned her eyes.

He'd opened his wound to let the toxin out. But there was still one more agonizing fact left. One more detail to reveal so he could move forward. It would be the last step in healing. She had to tell him his son's loss wasn't meaningless, that he'd helped her daughter. She had to thank him for his gift. Her gut was telling her now wasn't the time. But soon. And how would he take it? Would he close up again and go where no one could reach him?

He looked at her, and she made the mistake of looking back. The bottomless, gut-wrenching pain and loss in his gaze pierced her heart. Moisture gathered in her eyes, making his image waver in front of her. She felt a big fat tear spill over and slide down her cheek.

"Megan?" He straightened.

"I—don't mind me." She tried to laugh, but it sounded as if she was choking. This was so awful. She started to get up, but he gripped her arm, gently but firmly.

"Look at me."

Unable to say anything, she shook her head.

He cupped her face in his hands and forced her to meet his gaze while brushing the moisture from her cheeks with his thumbs. "Don't cry. Please. Not about me."

His gaze swept over her and he leaned in close. Her eyes drifted shut, and she waited to feel his lips. She ached for the touch of his mouth. Her heart pounded as she craved the sensation of a physical connection. She needed the closeness with him.

When it didn't happen, she opened her eyes. He looked tortured, but every female instinct she possessed told her it had nothing to do with his personal pain and everything to do with passion and desire. He rubbed his thumb across her mouth, then urged her just a fraction closer. And waited. She could feel his warm breath on her face.

Finally, she got the message. He had picked a heck of a time to start following the rules. She knew what he wanted. If she accepted his invitation, it would happen. The choice was hers. She could turn him away. But then she would never know what it felt like to make love with this man. And more than her next breath she wanted to know. So, really, there was no choice at all.

Chapter Ten

Simon waited, afraid she would back away. He'd never experienced longing as intense as what he felt for Megan. With every single, solitary fiber of his being, he wanted her to kiss him. The one the other day had unlocked this yearning, fueling the longing. Was it something about Megan? Or the fact that no one had really touched him since Marcus died.

Suddenly he felt a powerful, inescapable urge to connect with another human being. With Megan. Only Megan.

It was as if the trauma to his soul had bled over into his body, sending it into shock, allowing him to feel nothing. Megan had helped him recover on the outside. But somehow she'd managed to reach into his soul, to begin the healing process there, patiently nursing away the shock. For the first time in two years he wanted to touch and be touched. Feelings bombarded him, like an amusement park fun house with dizzying, potent sensations.

Why her? Why now? He didn't want to want her. He felt guilty that he did. But he could no more turn away from her than he could bring back his son. He almost wished Megan would stop him. Almost.

Somehow, confessing his sin had lifted a weight from someplace dark and deep inside him. He'd been so sure he would never feel anything but anguish for the rest of his life. It was as if he could finally breathe again. The earth hadn't stopped spinning and black clouds were parting to let the sun shine through. A stupid analogy. It was dumb. It was crazy. It was the God's honest truth.

He was like a drowning man who felt the grip of a rescuer's hand dragging him back from the deep, the touch of a savior's fingers pulling him back from the brink. All of a sudden his senses were pumped. He was on overload. Megan's eyes were the bluest blue he'd ever seen. Her hair was like spun gold. The sweet sound of her sigh fired him with desire. The touch of her hands made him ache in the most primal, elemental way. He wanted her.

And his instincts might have been in suspended animation, but they'd come back to life along with everything else. She wanted him, too.

Something had been sizzling between them from the moment he'd opened his eyes and thought she looked like an angel. In that moment, the fuse had been lit, ticking off the seconds until the explosion.

Time was up.

She touched her lips to his and he nearly came apart with the force of it. He tunneled his fingers into her hair and cupped her face between his palms, making the contact of their mouths more firm. His chest felt tight, as if he couldn't draw enough air into his lungs. His erection pressed painfully against the front of his pants. Megan moaned. Her hands were in his hair, on his shoulders, arms, neck, pulling at him as if she couldn't get close enough.

"Come upstairs with me." His words grated, rough and ragged, but he was on passion autopilot and beyond finesse.

Her movements stilled and he held his breath, afraid she would refuse him. He looked into her eyes. Her chest rose and fell rapidly, her breathing as harsh as his own. It seemed an eternity before she nodded.

"Yes," she whispered, and ran her tongue over her top lip.

The movement, so innocent, so erotic, made his heart pound faster and his need more urgent. He leaned down and unfastened the leg brace, letting it fall away. She stood up and held out her hand and he took it, wrapping her small fingers in his own. At the bottom of the stairs, she put her arm around his waist and they slowly climbed. Together.

At the top, they turned right. His room was large, spartan, with a king-size bed in the center and nightstands on either side. Across from it was a utilitarian oak dresser. To the left, the dressing area and bathroom.

Simon took her hand and led her to the side of the bed. Light from the hall kept the room from total blackness. He yanked the bedcovers back, baring the sheets.

He looked down at Megan. The last thing he wanted was more regrets. "Are you sure about this?"

Her eyes were huge but she nodded. "I'm sure. But I think—"

He touched a finger to her lips to silence her. "Simon says don't think. Just feel."

He leaned down and captured her lips with his and felt the shiver that rippled through her. Then he reached up and released the clip holding her hair, tossing it onto the nightstand. Golden strands spilled around her face and he ran his fingers through the silk.

"Beautiful," he breathed.

She settled her hands on his chest, then slowly slid them down to his waist until he held his breath in anticipation. But she pulled his shirt free and slipped her hands up underneath. Flattening her palms against his skin, she sighed with satisfaction.

"You feel—good."

"A poet," he teased.

The sensation of connection was something he couldn't describe. It felt better than anything he could remember. How long had it been since he'd touched and been touched? He grabbed the bottom of his T-shirt and yanked it off. He wanted to feel her heartbeat against his bare skin, the warmth of her body.

"Take off your top." He looked at her.

She stared back without moving, but a sparkle stole into her eyes. A playful, sweet, challenging, sexy-as-hell smile turned up the corners of her full mouth. When he caught on to her game, anticipation hummed through him, heating his blood.

"Simon says take off your top."

She reached down and yanked it over her head. From the waist up she wore a bra that was hardly more than scraps of white lace. He didn't think he'd ever seen a more beautiful sight in his life.

He stepped closer and their bodies barely brushed. With both hands, he reached behind her and unfastened the clasp, then hooked his fingers beneath the straps and dragged it off her shoulders to fall at their feet. He moved back just far enough to drink in the sight of her.

She was the most completely lovely thing he'd ever seen. All slender lines and feminine curves. He cupped her breasts in his hands and felt the perfect size and weight, flawless soft skin. A moan escaped her and her eyes drifted closed as her lips parted. She was sensuality incarnate and suddenly he wanted her naked. He wanted to see all of her.

"Simon says you have too many clothes on."

She smiled. "Megan says you first."

"That's not the way the game is played," he said, his mouth turning up.

"New rules."

"Okay. I'm easy." He released the fastener on his shorts. He stopped breathing when she took the zipper and dragged it down. Then he pushed off his briefs and shorts.

She kicked off her shoes and reached for her waistband, but he brushed her hands away. More than his next breath, he wanted to undress her the rest of the way. He slid his fingertips inside. With his eager assistance, all her remaining clothes began their descent. Along the way he brushed the soft, silken skin of her taut abdomen, the slender curve of her waist, the gentle roundness of her hips and thighs.

Finally she was standing before him naked as the day she was born and the sight of her took his breath away. He knew then that God must be a man. How else could he have created something so beautiful?

"You're a sight for sore eyes."

"Be still my heart."

Although her response was flip, Megan was far from offended. His words meant so much more because they came straight from the gut. Unrehearsed, unpracticed. Honest and sincere, they were like food to her famished soul. When he sat down on the side of the bed and held out his arms to her, she went into them without hesitation.

He encircled her waist and twisted, lowering her to the mattress. She squealed as the cold cotton sheets touched her skin.

"What?" he asked.

"A warning would have been nice. I think you keep these suckers in the freezer." She shivered.

"I'll warm you up." His whiskey-smooth tone made a promise his hands instantly started to keep. "Close your eyes."

Surprised, she stared at him.

"Simon says close your eyes." He smiled, a seductive satisfied expression.

Megan shivered again, but this time it wasn't the chill; it was expectation. This was the culmination of spending so many hours a day with this man and trying to resist him. The attraction arcing between them had become too strong to fight. Even if she wanted to, it felt too wonderful. His touch was like heaven to her lonely spirit. What could it hurt? For once, she refused to think about that question.

She did as he requested and closed her eyes, then felt the featherlight touch of his mouth on her eyelids, nose, cheeks and mouth. He traced the seam of her lips and she instantly opened to him. Taking what she offered, he invaded, stroking her until heat gathered inside her and spilled over, heating her from head to toe.

At the same time, his palm, resting on her belly, slid upward toward her breast. Anticipation grew. Awareness climbed. Then she felt the tip of his finger trace the peak just before he caught her nipple between his thumb and forefinger. It was like being zapped with a bolt of lightning and her eyes popped open.

"Simon says keep your eyes closed."

"But—"

"Simon says don't argue."

She closed her eyes and her mouth. Why argue when what he was doing felt better than anything she could remember in a very long time? Without sight, her other senses were heightened. He continued to trace her breast, around the peak, up her chest, along her neck, toying with her earlobe. Her breathing grew ragged and shallow. She wanted to feel his touch *everywhere.*

As if he could read her mind, he trailed down the center of her chest, skimmed her navel, then went lower, settling between her thighs. He parted her and found her most sensitive, feminine place. As he teased and rubbed, the sensation was too good for words and a moan slipped from her throat.

"I think we have a winner," he said, his voice filled with satisfaction.

"Yes," she breathed.

He smoothed and stroked, brushed and touched. Slow then fast and a pace in between. A knot coiled inside her. Pressure built, growing bigger, tighter, tenser. When she thought she couldn't stand any more, she finally went rigid, then shattered into a thousand points of light, pressing herself into his hand. It seemed like a lifetime before she was whole again.

Sighing, she opened her eyes and smiled weakly as she met Simon's satisfied gaze. "Wow."

"Good?"

"*Good* is such an inadequate word. But so right on," she said dreamily, her eyes drifting closed.

She felt something poking her in the thigh and looked at him. "Your turn."

"Hold that thought."

He reached into the nightstand beside him and fumbled for something. When he pulled it out, the foil package caught the light from the hall. Good Lord. Protection. She'd forgotten all about it.

"At least one of us is prepared," she said gratefully.

"Left over from a lifetime ago," he whispered.

He ripped open the package and, with shaking hands, settled the condom over himself then rolled it down. He eased between her legs, settling at the juncture of her thighs. In the dim light she could see the harsh intensity in his eyes, the tense set of his features.

"I haven't done this in a pretty long time. I don't know—"

This time she put her fingers over his mouth. "Simon said don't think, just feel. Shut up and kiss me."

One corner of his mouth lifted before he leaned down and did just that. His stubble scraped her chin, but she couldn't find the will to care. The sensation of their bodies touching, of being close, simply felt too good. Then he braced himself on his elbows. With one thrust, he was inside her and too good turned into too wonderful.

He sucked in a breath and closed his eyes, an expression of concentrated wonder on his face. With excruciating slowness, he withdrew to just the point of protest, then entered her again. Over and over he repeated the motion, advance and retreat until he urged her higher and higher.

Suddenly he stopped. His whole body tensed as he threw back his head. With a guttural groan, he thrust one last time, then his body went rigid with his release. Megan was right behind him, free-falling as the pleasure overtook her. When their afterquakes ceased, he eased himself from between her thighs and lay on his back, gathering her close while their breathing returned to normal.

He dropped a quick kiss on her lips, then sat up, leaving her for several moments as he disappeared into the bathroom. It was long enough for sanity to return and the cold along with it. The floaty feeling vanished, and she hit the ground with a very big thud. She was falling all right, in more ways than one.

Megan gathered up her clothes and slipped into them before going downstairs into the powder room. She turned on the light and locked the door behind her. In the mirror over the sink, she saw the shell-shocked expression on her face and the realization hit her with the force of a two-by-four.

She'd just slept with her patient.

It didn't matter that the activity hadn't aggravated the healing injuries from his accident. Or that he'd been a more than willing participant, encouraging her with his magic hands and gifted lips. She'd been completely and utterly swept away. Consequences hadn't once entered her mind. All she could think about was wanting Simon and how much he'd wanted her back. But she was a health-care professional—*his* health-care professional. How could she have let this happen?

There was only one thing she could do.

She splashed water over her face, then dried it on the hand towel. Taking a deep breath, she unlocked the door and braced herself to face the music.

Simon was dressed and waiting for her, standing without either crutch by the fireplace. "Hi."

"Hi."

"I can't help noticing you're wearing clothes. Does that mean you're not staying?"

She walked to the sofa table beside him and picked up her purse and medical bag. "I have to go."

He folded his arms over his chest. "Bayleigh's with her grandparents having a sleepover. I thought we could, too. It would save you the trip back in the morning."

"Come on, Simon. Who are you trying to kid?" She inched closer to the front door. "You don't need me any longer. I think you can take care of yourself just fine."

"You couldn't be more wrong."

"This is me," she said, touching a finger to her chest. Her heart was pounding. "I was there a little while ago. Physically you were—"

"What?"

Pretty amazing, she wanted to say. Awfully wonderful. Sexy, sweet and so very wrong for her. "Let's just say that as a nurse there's nothing more you need from me. I'm not coming back."

"Why?"

"You're brighter than the average bear. I think you can figure it out."

"Because we made love?"

"Bingo."

"What if I said it won't happen again?"

"Will it?"

"If there's a God in heaven," he said.

"That's why. It's completely unprofessional. I'm a day late and a dollar short getting my career off the ground. Something like this could tank it before I ever get started. I love what I do, Simon. I've worked too long and too hard to get where I am. It can't happen again. And I can't trust you."

"I'd like to point out that I didn't kiss you."

"Did so," she said, feeling like an idiot.

But the memory of his mouth on hers, and the things he'd made her feel, robbed her of coherent thought. Not to mention the betraying heat spreading through her again. It wasn't him she was afraid of. It was herself. Where he was concerned, she was spineless. She let out a long breath.

"Okay. Strictly speaking I kissed you. But it's a technicality. You broke the essence of the rule by invading my personal space. Touching me. Being sweet—"

"So take me out back and beat the crap out of me. But don't go." He ground out the last two words from between clenched teeth.

Megan studied him and saw—desolation. His mouth pulled into a straight line and the angles and planes of his face seemed jagged, harsh, chiseled from stone. Deep lines were carved along either side of his nose and mouth. But his eyes snapped blue fire. That was something, at least. When she'd seen him that first night in the ER, there'd been no life in his gaze.

When she'd agreed to be his home nurse, she'd rationalized that it was an opportunity to sort out and put to bed the feelings he'd evoked. She never planned to literally go to bed with him. If anything, her feelings about him were even more confusing. But there was no point in sorting them out. She had a child to think about, to support.

She met his gaze. "If there's even the suggestion of impropriety between nurse and patient, I could lose my job. What happened between us was more than a suggestion."

He made a dismissive noise. "What's really going on, Megan? What can I say to talk you out of this?"

"Nothing. I have to go. Take care of yourself, Simon. I've enjoyed knowing you. Thanks for—"

"For what?" Anger pulled his mouth into a straight line and settled in his eyes as he took a step toward her. "You're the one who got me back on my feet. You have nothing to thank me for."

To quote him, he couldn't be more wrong. He'd done everything for her daughter, and she owed him. He'd finally taken the first steps back and was on his way. But this still wasn't the time to say her thanks.

He ran a hand through his hair. "You're hiding behind the job. This—something—is between you and me. We both know I'm no victim. I did start it. Because I wanted you. I want you now, and I'd bet everything I have or ever hope to have that you want me, too. So tell me, Megan. What are you running from?"

She didn't even want to go there. All she'd wanted was to let him know how grateful she was. She hadn't actually said the words but didn't actions speak louder?

Before the thought could sink in that there wasn't enough thanks in the world, she grabbed her sweater from the stairway post opposite the front door. "I have to go. Don't take this the wrong way, but I never want to see you in my emergency room again."

"Megan—"

"Goodbye, Simon."

She walked out and hurried down the sidewalk to her car. Her mission was half accomplished. Simon was opening up. She hadn't thanked him personally. One out of two wasn't bad. But she just couldn't stay. For someone who was just beginning to flex his emotional muscles again, he'd sure nailed her. She *was* running. As fast as she could. And it had nothing to do with losing her job and everything to do with losing her heart. But she hadn't reached the point of no return.

She'd gotten out just in time.

Chapter Eleven

Megan walked into the hospital cafeteria and helped herself to a diet soda and a piece of fruit. While she waited in line to pay, she looked around the nearly empty room. After terminating her assignment with Simon the day before, she'd managed to pick up a per diem shift. So far it was a slow day in the ER. But she spotted a familiar face at a table by the window.

After paying the cashier for her items, she wandered across the room to a circular table surrounded by four orange plastic chairs on silver metal frames. "Mind if I join you?"

Startled, Janet glanced up. Then she smiled warmly. "Megan. Of course. Sit down."

"Thanks." Outside the window, there was a courtyard filled with sculpted bushes, plants, trees and flowers. A stepping stone path led to wrought-iron tables, chairs and benches. Through the branches, sunlight and blue sky winked down. It was a tranquil and lovely view and she could understand why Janet had picked this spot.

After settling herself, Megan cut her apple into slivers and surgically removed the core and pits. "What are you doing here?"

"I got beeped."

"Oh."

Megan remembered her friend was a volunteer liaison between doctors and families in handling consent, procurement and distribution of lifesaving organs for a number of hospitals in the Los Angeles area. For one week a month, Janet made herself available twenty-four hours a day to support any family who had lost a loved one. She was there for comfort and to answer any questions.

"Did they call you in about the teenage girl in the car accident?" Megan asked.

Sadness and exhaustion made Janet look older. "Yes. Single car. Massive head injuries. Her EEG is flat. Machines are keeping her body alive while the family considers the options."

Megan reached over and took her hand, squeezing it reassuringly. "They're lucky to have you. You're the best."

The older woman sighed. "I know."

"And humble, too."

"You know me too well." She smiled and a little of her spirit seemed to return. "What are you doing here?"

"The ER was shorthanded."

"But I didn't think your assignment with Simon was over yet. Is he fully recovered?"

Megan had a feeling his powers of recovery were pretty amazing—in more ways than one. But last night she'd left before she could find out for sure. And none of that was something she wanted to share.

She took a sip of her soda, then shifted uncomfortably in her chair. "He can take care of himself now."

"You quit, didn't you?"

"I'm not exactly sure how you came to that conclusion based on my comment."

"As you said, I'm the best. I'm right, too, aren't I?"

She hesitated, then met the other woman's gaze. "Yes."

"Why, Megan? I thought things were going well."

"Depends on your definition of well. He did open up a bit."

"That's good." Janet sat up straighter as she toyed with the teaspoon resting on the saucer beneath her coffee cup. "What did he tell you?"

"About the divorce. He said his business required him to put in a lot of hours and there was travel involved."

The other woman nodded. "He was gone a lot. Donna often mentioned it. But she had a hard time making a life for herself. Did he say anything else?"

"I don't think he intended to tell me, but he said they died together in the accident. He blames himself."

"Still?" Janet shook her head.

Megan nodded. "He said it was his weekend to take Marcus and if he hadn't put business first, his son would still be alive."

"That's good." She leaned closer, her gaze piercing. "No?"

"Yes. If he'd volunteered the information freely."

"How did you get him to open up?"

"I kept hammering away until he pushed back by asking about my relationship with Bayleigh's father. But I think the fact that he brought her up at all is hopeful. Then I touched a nerve and he blew up."

Janet nodded. "Did he talk about Donna and Marcus—

donating their organs, I mean? Did he say anything about how he feels about it?''

Megan shook her head. A vision of Simon from last night filled her mind. His sorrow and grief etched in the lines of his face. He'd been dealing with the remembered pain of losing his son. And then they'd gotten sidetracked. She would never know if he'd have freely offered that part of his pain.

''He didn't say anything about it. Period.'' But Megan had nagging concerns in that regard. ''And that's what worries me, Jan. You and I have talked about this. For so many families the healing process starts with the decision to donate organs. It's been two years. I don't understand. If Simon gave consent for organ donation—''

Janet's expression was bleak. ''He didn't make the decision. I did.''

''You never told me that,'' Megan said, stunned.

''It didn't seem necessary. He refused to see you when you wanted to meet with him.'' She sighed and shook her head, remembering. ''He was on a plane on his way overseas when the accident happened. I couldn't get in touch with him right away. After the divorce, Donna gave me power of attorney, just in case. But I never thought I'd have to use it. You know as well as I do there's only a small window of time when the organs are viable enough to do any good. I watch people struggle with the decision for so many reasons. I didn't. It was so clear to me. It was a way to somehow make sense of senseless loss.''

Megan nodded. ''I know.''

''But Simon didn't have a chance to take those steps with me. By the time he was able to get home, it was done and he didn't understand.''

''He didn't approve of what you did?'' Megan held

her breath. If she didn't draw in air, maybe she wouldn't feel the fear, pain and desolation she knew were scratching to be let in.

Janet shook her head. "That's putting it mildly. He was so angry. Suffice it to say the last thing he wanted was to meet people who were living and asking to thank him for something he didn't support. A part of him died when he lost Marcus. I blame myself for—"

"No. Don't go there, Jan. With all my heart I believe someday he will understand why you did what you did."

"I hoped when he reached out to you that he was finally getting there. That soon he would be able to put the past to rest and move on. It sounds as if you were making progress. What happened, Megan? What did he do to make you quit?"

It wasn't him, she wanted to say. It was herself. "That doesn't matter. What's important is that I believe he's started the process of coming back."

"How do you know? What makes you think so?"

"There were—signs." Physical signs that were pretty hard to ignore. And she hadn't.

"You need to go back to him."

As she stared into her soda, Megan felt the other woman's hand on her arm. She looked up. "Why me?"

"I don't have an answer for that. But I do know for two years he's withdrawn from life. And I think his dangerous hobbies are taking him further and further away. I'm worried about him. For some reason you got through and he reached out. I believe you're the only one who can pull him back from the edge."

Megan recalled what he'd said that night in the ER. Living on the edge was the only safe place to feel anything. His revelations last night had given her a small window of understanding about what he'd meant.

Megan shook her head. "I can't be the one. You've got to trust me on this. There's a good explanation for why I can't go back."

"Did you sleep with him?"

Stunned, Megan could only stare at the other woman.

"I'll take that as a yes," Janet said wryly.

"How do you do that?"

"It's a gift. I have a feeling it's one of the signs you were talking about. And I agree it's hopeful. To the best of my knowledge, there hasn't been anyone for him since the accident. I've kept in close contact with him."

"There must have been someone. He had—" Megan felt heat climb into her cheeks.

"Protection?" Janet smiled as she leaned back in her chair.

"Yes." Megan focused on the other woman's face as images of heat and need and instinct tumbled through her mind. The closeness. How good she'd felt in his arms. "Are they good after so long? Is there a condom shelf life?"

Janet laughed. "That's out of my sphere of expertise. Did it break?"

Megan's cheeks, just beginning to cool, flamed again. "I don't know. I left as fast as I could."

"And you don't want to go back." The older woman sighed. "Because obviously you're attracted to him. You're not the sort to hop into the sack with just any warm body."

"Thank you, I think." She met Janet's gaze. "He said I'm the rainbows and moonlights type."

"You are. A romantic. Looking for love. This is better than I could have hoped."

Megan thought Janet couldn't be more wrong. It was the worst thing that could happen.

Her friend's expression turned serious. "He finally reached out, Megan. Without you I'm not sure he'll have a reason to finish the process you've started."

"But don't you see? I don't want to be his reason. I have to think about Bayleigh—first, last, always."

"Isn't there a chance that you and Simon can—"

Megan shook her head. "Not a chance. And you know why better than anyone. I want to give my daughter a family. Usually that consists of a father, mother and a child. Even if he could get past the fact that my child can see because his child is gone, why would he want to care about anyone that much ever again?"

"Did he tell you that?"

"No. But—"

"So you're assuming. You're assigning him feelings he hasn't actually expressed. There's only one reason you would do that, Megan."

"And what would that be?"

Janet leaned her forearms on the table. "You're afraid to care about anyone, too."

"Have you been taking those classes again?" she accused.

"That's what Simon always says when I nail him."

"You didn't nail me." She didn't want to think about the fact that she and Simon had anything in common.

Janet looked at her watch, then stood abruptly. "I'd love to debate this with you, but I have to get back to ICU."

"Okay." Megan felt like a slug. In her own distress and confusion, she'd forgotten why the other woman was there in the first place.

"Megan? Don't abandon him. There's still the matter of telling him how Bayleigh's sight was saved."

Megan watched the older woman dispose of her trash

then leave the cafeteria. She didn't have to tell Simon anything. He didn't want to know. He didn't approve. She was glad she hadn't said a word about it.

Because the fact that she missed him so much was her own sign. A sign that she was starting to care. And the best possible reason for her to be relieved that she'd quit. Last night she'd thought she'd gotten out in the nick of time. She still believed that with all her heart.

Simon stood outside the door to Megan's apartment. It had been easy to find her. He already knew she was in the phone book, and there weren't a lot of Brightwells.

He looked around the outside of the well-manicured complex. It was a security building, but he'd been going in as someone was coming out and they'd held the gate for him. Good thing he wasn't a serial killer. Bad that he felt twinges of an unwelcome protective streak for Megan.

He knocked and instantly heard running feet. Through the door he heard a little girl's voice.

"Who's there?"

"Simon," he answered.

"Mommy's patient? The one with the hurt leg?"

He looked down at his jeans. Without the brace he could finally wear them and do without crutches. Although he expected to catch hell from his nurse about it. "Yes. I'm your mommy's patient with the hurt leg. We talked on the phone. When you had a pj day. Remember?"

The door opened and Megan's little angel-in-training stood there. "I remember."

A sharp pain stabbed him as he looked at this beautiful, living, breathing child. Her golden hair was cut in a bob around her small face. She was wearing navy stretch pants with flowers and a solid navy sweatshirt with a turtleneck underneath. Curious, solemn blue eyes regarded him from behind wire-rimmed glasses.

"Hi, Bayleigh," he said.

"Hi. You know my name."

"Your mom told me. Is she home?"

She nodded and her hair shimmered in the sunlight. "She's got music on because she hates cleaning her room. She says it helps her go faster."

He heard the music and the vacuum, which explained why she hadn't answered his knock. Something told him she wouldn't be too happy about him standing here talking to her daughter.

"Does your mom let you answer the door to strangers?"

"No. But I asked who was there, and you're not a stranger. We talked on the phone."

He couldn't fault her logic. "Can I come in?"

"How do you ask?"

He felt another slice in his heart. It was a question he'd always ask Marcus, when he'd taught his son the magic words "please" and "thank you." He pushed the thought away. "Please?"

She shook her head so hard strands of hair covered her face, and she brushed them away. "Don't you remember the game?"

"Ah," he said, nodding. He smiled. "Simon says may I come in?"

"Yes, you may." She gave him a radiant smile and stepped aside, opening the door wide.

"Thank you." He passed her, and she shut the door behind him.

"You're welcome."

The first-floor apartment was warm, homey and so

very Megan-like. There were pictures everywhere, which was why she had probably noticed he didn't have any. Collages of them lined the wall, as well as photos of Bayleigh at various ages. On the end tables flanking the beige floral sofa, pictures in all kinds of frames littered the tops. Stuffed animals rested on either end of the sofa back. There was an entertainment center on the wall opposite the couch with kids' movies displayed. Straight ahead, he saw a dinette in the alcove off the kitchen. And a hall he figured led to her bedroom.

The room with her bed. Just the thought of it sent the blood surging hot through his veins heading due south. This was just one of the numerous downsides of coming back to life, he thought ruefully as the heaviness settled in his groin.

"You have a nice place here," he said.

She glanced around. "Mommy says it's perfect for the two of us. She says it's her and me against the world."

Simon looked at her small face, the glasses that gave her the mature air to go with the grown-up sentiment. "I like your glasses."

"Thank you. Mommy said my eyes were broken, but the doctor fixed them and now I have to wear glasses to see better."

The announcement stunned him. He knew she was in kindergarten, which made her about five—two years younger than Marcus would be if he'd lived. She talked about it as if she had no memory of the event. "Do you remember when the doctor fixed them?"

She shrugged. "Not much. I was little then. But Mommy says I look smart."

"I think you look pretty."

"I think you're pretty smart," she said, giggling.

He laughed along with her and felt something inside

him crack and fall away. The ice around his heart? He shook his head. Way too poetic for him. He saw a movement in his peripheral vision.

"Bayleigh, it's time for you— Oh!"

Simon could almost hear the screeching halt as Megan entered the living room and came to a sudden full and complete stop. "Hi."

"What are you doing here?" She came closer and nestled her daughter close to her side. Protectively close. "Bay, you know better than to open the door to a stranger."

"It's Simon, Mom."

"Yes, I know. But—"

"We played Simon says, and he said it right so I had to let him in."

"No—" She huffed out a breath as she slid a nervous glance in his direction. "We'll talk about it later."

Bayleigh pushed her glasses up on her nose as she looked at her mother. He remembered what Megan had said about her daughter seeing the eye doctor to get a checkup and her strong negative reaction when he'd suggested rescheduling. He wondered how serious the child's eye problems were. Serious enough to make her father leave when she and Megan had needed him most? He recalled what she'd said the other night about just getting her career off the ground. Had the child's problem been so severe, Megan had put everything on hold?

"Mommy, I think you're the best nurse in the whole wide world."

With her arm around the child's shoulders, Megan grinned down at her. "Besides the fact that you're in deep doo-doo, why do you think that?"

Bayleigh pointed at him. "He's all better."

"And you know this—how?" her mother asked, glancing at him.

"He's walkin' all by himself."

Megan met his gaze. "Good point, Bay. But with Simon, I mean Mr. Reynolds—"

"Too late," he said. "We've already progressed to first names. Right, Bayleigh?"

"Right, Simon." She nodded vehemently.

"With him," Megan continued, "the fact that he's walking without crutches and a leg brace doesn't necessarily mean I'm a good nurse. It could just mean he's not following doctor's orders."

"But, Mommy—"

"You know what, sweetie? Didn't you promise to put away your dolls and the clothes and the playhouse furniture?"

"But, Mo-om—"

Megan put her hands on the little girl's shoulders and turned her toward the hall. "March, young lady."

She whirled around. "But, Mom, you didn't say it right."

He couldn't stop the smile turning up the corners of his mouth. "Simon says clean up your room."

"Okay." The little girl smiled back, then turned toward the hall. She stopped and glanced over her shoulder. "But don't leave before I get finished."

He met her gaze, then looked at Megan. "I'll do my best."

When the child was gone and the clatter of toys being moved around drifted to him, he let out a long breath. "She's something else."

"Yes, she is." Megan's expression softened as she looked at the hallway where her daughter had been only a moment before.

"Isn't she young to be wearing glasses?"

Her head snapped around so fast he thought she would get whiplash. "What?" she asked sharply.

"Why does she have to wear glasses?"

"Why does anyone? The corrective lenses improve her vision."

Based on what Bayleigh had innocently told him and Megan's reaction just now, he was getting vibes that he was right about the child's eyes. "Why does she need the corrective lenses? Does it have anything to do with why the jerk walked out on you both?"

"Simon, I—"

"Don't sidestep me, Megan. Is that why he left?"

"Yes," she said, her mouth trembling. "She had a condition when she was born. It's—the name is too long to remember. But the bottom line is she could have gone blind."

"She told me the doctor fixed her eyes."

Megan nodded. She hesitated as if deciding what to say. "She had surgery. Now she wears glasses," she finished simply.

"Why didn't you tell me?"

"Why did you think I should?" she said defensively, but she didn't look at him directly. "I'm a nurse. You're my patient. Were," she added.

"You know, I've had it up to here with you and this whole personal, professional thing you do to put up roadblocks as you run from the truth."

"I can't help what you're fed up with."

She didn't deny the whole running-away thing or the detours. Maybe because she was hyperaware that she was doing it. Because she was starting to care and didn't want to. Simon knew all about that. Megan was single-handedly responsible for the fact that he was back in the land of the living. Like it or not, whether he wanted to or not, he was feeling again.

He ran his fingers through his hair. "We went way beyond professional a week ago."

"And because I am a professional, it shouldn't have happened."

"I'm not going to argue the right or wrong of it with you. The fact is it did happen. And you ran away. I thought we were friends."

"I'm your nurse."

He shook his head. "You quit."

"You should be happy I'm saving your insurance company some money. Besides you're getting around pretty well without the brace and crutches."

"The leg is a little sore, but I'm on the mend."

"Good. So we agree you don't need a nurse. Why did you track me down, Simon?"

He might not need a nurse, but he needed a friend. "I got used to you bossing me around."

"You missed me," she said.

"Like a toothache."

She laughed. "Has anyone ever told you that writing greeting cards wouldn't be a good career move for you?"

"No."

"When you reach out and touch someone it's with a two-by-four."

It was no secret to anyone, least of all him, that his interpersonal-relationship radar was rusty. But he would bet she'd run because she was just as afraid as he was of caring about someone. The saturated fat in the veins of her life.

That didn't mean he couldn't return the favor and help her. Maybe he could do her some good and show her that not all men were heartless jerks. He wouldn't walk out when she needed him most. He wished he could go back to his fringe existence, back to not feeling. But Megan had coaxed him out. God help him, he just couldn't go back into the dark after basking in her light.

"Why did you track me down, Simon?" she asked again.

"You're wrong about me not needing you. But not as a nurse, Megan. As my friend."

Her eyes widened in surprise. "I don't know—"

"You said you wanted me to live again. That's what I'm trying to do. Help me, Megan."

He could see the struggle in her eyes. And something else he couldn't name. Fear maybe? Before he could figure out what, she released a long breath. Whatever conflict she'd had, it was over and she'd given in.

"Okay. Friends." She pointed at him. "But—"

He put his hands on his hips and grinned. "Here it comes."

"What?"

"The rules."

"Yeah." She smiled back. "Not that it does any good with you. But for what it's worth, friends don't have sex."

"What's sex, Mommy?"

Simon grinned. How could you not love a kid who picked that moment to walk in the room? He couldn't wait to see Miss-I've-got-an-answer-for-everything deal with the question.

Chapter Twelve

Megan froze and so did her brain. Think fast. Sex? Sounded like…

''Six,'' she said. ''I said six, the age you'll be on your next birthday.''

Bayleigh pushed her glasses up more firmly on her nose. ''Why would you say no six?''

Megan looked at Simon, who appeared to be enjoying her discomfiture far too much, judging by the twinkle in his blue eyes. And the way his mouth turned up slightly told her he wanted to laugh. All she could think about was how much she wished to feel his mouth on hers.

Focus, she ordered herself. She cleared her throat then stared at her daughter. ''I said six because—''

''Because,'' Simon jumped in when she hesitated. ''I was telling your mom that I thought the two of you should come to my town house sometime and go fishing but I didn't think you were old enough. I thought you were going to be five on your next birthday. She said 'no six.'''

''Fishing?'' Bayleigh said, her eyes growing wide.

Megan moved beside him and let out a long breath. ''Good save,'' she whispered. ''Bay, you're not interested in fishing, are you?''

''Sure, I am.'' She put her hands on her hips. ''Uncle Dan keeps promising to take me, but he always has to work.''

''But, sweetie,'' she said. ''It can be pretty boring and you have to put yucky stuff like worms on the end of a hook.''

''No worms. Fish eggs,'' Simon said.

''Are they like the eggs Mommy breaks into the pancake batter?''

Simon moved close to her and went down on one knee. ''No. Or we can use cheese and ham.''

''With bread? Like sandwiches?''

''No. The bread would come apart in the water.''

To his credit, Simon remained absolutely as serious as Bayleigh. How was it possible to resist a man like that? She had to find a way, because when he learned the truth, it could break her child's heart, as well as her own.

''Is fishing boring?'' Bayleigh asked him.

''I don't think so. But if *you* do, we could stop and look for shells on the beach.''

Bayleigh turned the I-want-to-go-now look on her. ''When are we goin' fishing with Simon, Mom?''

Uh-oh. ''I'm not sure. We all have busy schedules—''

''I don't,'' he said. ''Remember, I have no job.''

Megan glanced from her daughter's guileless expression to Simon's pretending-to-be-innocent-while-backing-her-into-a-corner look.

"Do you live under the freeway in a box?" Bayleigh asked, worry pulling her forehead into a frown.

"No. I have a town house at the beach. Why would you think that?"

"Because sometimes I ask Mommy to stay home with me and she always says she has to work. If she doesn't earn money we'll have to live in a box underneath the freeway."

"I was joking, Bay," Megan hurried to explain. "You know that."

"Yeah, but if Simon doesn't have a job, how can he have any money for a house? Or food? Or clothes? I never met anyone who didn't have a job before."

Megan glanced at Simon, who had a pretty good frown of his own going on. "It's not polite to ask questions, Bay."

"But you always tell me to ask if I don't understand. What does Simon do all day? I go to school. Grampy is a doctor. Grammy stays home. Mommy works. Uncle Dan goes to the office. Aunt Cassie is a nurse like Mommy. And Uncle Kyle is a—I can't 'member."

"Attorney," Megan supplied.

The little girl nodded. "Everybody does somethin'. How does he earn money? What does he do all day? Fish?"

Simon cleared his throat. "Sometimes grown-ups work very hard and make a lot of money to put in the bank. Then they have enough to live on and don't have to go to a job every day."

Bayleigh looked up at him. "Did you do that, Simon?"

"Yeah. I have plenty of money."

The worry lines in her face disappeared. "I'm glad. So when can we go fishin'?"

Megan jammed her hands into the pockets of her jeans. ''Bayleigh, why don't you let me talk to Simon about this while you go finish putting your toys away.''

''I'm already finished, Mom. You're just trying to get rid of me so you can talk to Simon alone.''

''Is that true, Megan?'' His frown had disappeared, too, replaced by the insufferable look he wore when he was sure he had the upper hand. ''Are you trying to get me alone?''

''No.'' But of course the heat flaring in her cheeks told him something else. ''Look, we can't just drop everything and go to the beach.''

''Why not?'' Simon asked.

''Yeah, why not?'' Bayleigh looked up at him, and he met her gaze and smiled.

Two against one. And she was weakening. ''Because we've got grocery shopping to do. Errands to run. I've only got two days off and—''

''You're not working this weekend?'' he asked.

''No,'' she reluctantly confirmed.

The man was far too sharp and flustered her far too much. She'd agreed to be his friend. It was the least she could do. But she didn't want to involve Bayleigh. Somehow he'd worked his way into her life and now he was charming her daughter, too. How did she get out of this without looking like her heart was three sizes too small?

''How about this?'' he said. ''I'll help you get all your chores out of the way today. And tomorrow we'll go fishing.''

''Ya-ay.'' Bayleigh clapped her hands together and jumped up and down. ''Simon says we're goin' fishing.''

''What do you say, Megan?''

Remembering her own game of Simon says, her insides quivered and her heart pounded painfully. The man was a devil. Basically, he'd left her no choice—unless she wanted to disappoint her daughter.

But it would be just this once. The child had been let down too many times in her five years. And it was clear she wanted a father. Megan couldn't let Bayleigh set her sights on Simon or there would be another very big letdown in her future. First and foremost, Megan vowed to protect her little girl. Everything else came second, including her own happiness.

"I say—thank you very much."

Sunday morning Simon whistled as he returned from the grocery store and lugged the bags from the bottom level where he had parked his car to the main floor of the town house. He had to take it slow because of the leg, but that didn't dampen his spirits. It had been a long time since he'd whistled. Hell, he couldn't remember the last time he'd looked forward to anything as much as he was anticipating Megan and Bayleigh's visit today.

He'd gone to the market for food, in case the little girl got hungry. After Marcus died, he'd avoided even looking at his son's favorites. Seeing the familiar crackers, fruit snacks and packaged juices had opened the wound in his heart. It hurt like a son of a gun, but he'd made himself pick up the items. He had no idea what Bayleigh's choices would be, but there was a good chance she'd like some of the same things Marcus had.

He was looking forward to seeing her. And her mother.

Every time Megan ran away, he got another dose of what lonely felt like and he didn't care for it. Still, he couldn't blame her. She'd been abandoned by a guy she trusted. No one knew better than him how excruciating it was to move forward when life kicked you in the teeth. But he was determined to prove she could trust him.

Not an easy assignment when he wanted so badly to pull her into his arms and kiss her until they were both breathless and burning with need. But she'd warned him about the rules. He grinned again at how that had bitten her in the backside with Bayleigh's innocent question. He patted himself on the back for the way he'd saved her bacon, then used it to his own advantage. No way would he have gotten Megan to agree to this outing without her daughter's dogged assistance. And he very much wanted to see the two of them.

Just as he finished putting groceries away, he heard the doorbell chime.

"Saved by the bell," he said.

Anticipation mixed with exhilaration as he walked down the hall from the kitchen to the front door. When he opened it, he was surprised to see Janet.

"Hey," he said. "What are you doing here?"

"Nice to see you, too," she said. "I came to check up on you. The last time I was here, you weren't in the mood for visitors."

He remembered that day. Was it only a couple of weeks ago? He'd been in pain and not just the physical kind. But he winced when he recalled how surly he'd been to Janet.

"Come on in."

"Thank you." She passed in front of him and into the room, where she sat down on the sofa. After closing the door, he joined her.

She looked him over. "I see you're doing better. The hospitality fairy must have sprinkled you with friendly dust."

He sighed. "About the other day—I'm sorry. I was rude, and it was inexcusable."

"You left out cranky and impossible."

''That, too.'' He rubbed a hand over his neck. ''Can I get you something to drink?''

''No. I don't want to let you off the hook just yet. I like you this way,'' she said, a smile turning up the corners of her mouth.

''What way?''

''Squirming. Who do I need to thank for this miracle?''

''Megan Brightwell.'' Something flickered in Janet's eyes, and he could have sworn it was an effort for her not to react. Then the look was gone, and he figured he'd imagined it.

''Who is she?''

''A nurse. I met her in the ER the night of the accident. She works there per diem when she's not doing a shift for a home health-care company. I pulled some strings and—''

''Translation—you threw a tantrum,'' she interjected.

''Okay. Anyway, she's been my nurse for the past couple of weeks.''

''Then I want some of whatever she's been giving you.''

What had she been giving him? No slack for one thing. Straight talk, toughness with a healthy dose of tenderness tossed in. And understanding. As if she had a direct line to his demons. The combination was irresistible. But there were still some things that bedeviled him. Things he'd never discussed with Janet. At least not civilly. About what happened after the accident that took his son and her daughter.

''She has a little girl. Bayleigh. Sweet kid.''

''You've met her?'' Janet asked.

He nodded. ''To make a long story short, and for reasons I'm not going to tell you, I tracked Megan down at home. The little girl answered the door.''

''Really?''

''Apparently she had a tough time after she was born. Something with her eyes that could have left her blind.''

''How awful.''

''The worst part is her father walked out on both of them when the going got tough.''

''Imbecile,'' she said angrily.

''Yeah. Anyway, I've been wondering about—Marcus.''

Surprise flickered in her eyes. ''What about him?''

''After he—you said you were going to try to contact the recipients of his organs. Did you?''

''Some of them,'' she admitted. ''And the people Donna helped.''

''Do you ever feel that Donna's in pieces?''

Janet shook her head. ''My memory is of a beautiful, vibrant woman whose life had meaning. Because of her, the father who got her heart can spend more time with his wife and five children. The man who received her corneas will be able to see his first grandchild. The young mother with her kidneys can raise the baby she risked her life to bring into the world. That's what I think about.''

He nodded as he mulled over her words. He couldn't help thinking about Bayleigh. Her eyes were broken and the doctor fixed them. Now she wore glasses. And she was in kindergarten. While Megan finally moved ahead with the career she'd put on hold. Thanks to the miracle of modern medicine.

''Did you meet anyone who received Marcus's organs?''

Janet folded her hands and rested them in her lap. "Yes, I did."

"His corneas?" When she nodded, he asked, "Boy or girl?"

"Girl."

"How old?" He rested his elbows on his knees, then shook his head. "No. I don't want to know."

She hesitated, then said, "All right."

"Have you kept in touch with all the people you've met through Donna—and Marcus?"

She shrugged. "Some of them, the ones who want to continue the connection. Others want to put it behind them and go on in as normal a fashion as possible."

"What about the little girl?" He'd thought the idea of it would open up the ache inside. And it did. But not as much as he'd expected.

"Yes. I still see her." She looked down at the linked hands in her lap, then met his gaze. "The family has always wanted to thank you. I could arrange a meeting between you and—"

He shook his head. "Maybe someday. But not yet."

"All right. If you change your mind, let me know." She studied him. "But for what it's worth, I haven't seen you like this in—well, longer than I can remember. You look—"

"How?"

"It's hard to describe." She shook her head. "Not content exactly. And not happy precisely. Just—as if you're looking forward to something."

"That's because I am."

"I'm going out on a limb here. Does it have something to do with Megan?"

"And her daughter," he confirmed. "They're coming over, and I'm taking Bayleigh fishing." He glanced at the clock on the dining room wall. ''In fact, they should be here any minute. When you rang the bell, I was sure it was them.''

Janet stood up abruptly. ''Look at the time. I've got to run.''

Surprised, he looked at her again. ''You just got here. Stick around and I'll introduce you to the woman who's responsible for changing me from a cranky ingrate to the man you see before you.''

''I—I wish I could, Simon, but I just remembered I've got an appointment.'' She grabbed her purse from the coffee table and headed for the door. ''Another time. I'd love to meet her.''

''Okay.'' He got up and followed her.

She opened the door and walked out. ''Bye,'' she called over her shoulder.

''See you—'' But her car door slammed as the word ''later'' came out.

''Hi. Sorry we're late,'' Megan said when Simon answered her knock on the door.

''No problem. Hi, Bayleigh.''

''Hi.''

''Come in,'' he said.

Megan walked in, but her child stood there like a statue and looked up at him. He grinned at her. ''Simon says come in.''

Bayleigh took a big step over the threshold. Pushing her glasses up, she asked, ''When are we goin' fishin'?''

''Bayleigh. That's not polite.'' Megan met his gaze. ''Sorry.''

He held up two fingers. ''That's two sorrys in less than a minute. One more and I go skateboarding down that big hill on the 405 freeway. The sun is out. The sky is blue. We're going to have fun. Right?" he asked, looking at the little girl.

"Right." She nodded emphatically. "Simon says no more sorrys."

"Okay, then."

When he met her gaze, a wolfish gleam stole into his eyes, sending a sizzle of awareness through Megan. In the car on the way over, Bay had chattered incessantly about two subjects: being a pilgrim in the kindergarten program the following week and catching fish with cheese. Mostly it was fish, liberally sprinkled with comments starting with Simon this or Simon that. Her daughter's little body had practically vibrated with excitement. Megan's had hummed for a very different reason. What had happened the last time she'd been here wasn't ever far from her mind. But it wouldn't happen again, especially today with her little chaperone along. Still, she couldn't relax.

"Follow me," he said, leading the way downstairs.

"Where we goin'?"

"To get supplies," Simon answered.

"I get to be a pilgrim at school," the little girl said. "The day before Thanksgiving."

Bringing up the rear, Megan couldn't hear his reply. But that didn't bother her as much as her normally shy child sharing details of her life so unselfconsciously. She wanted a family almost as badly as Megan yearned to give her one. But getting attached to Simon wasn't a good idea—for either of them. Megan still had to tell him the truth about Bay's cornea surgery. When she did, the last thing he would want was the two of them.

And the two of them wouldn't be here if he hadn't helped her out of a jam yesterday. But she wouldn't have been in hot water in the first place if he hadn't showed up. Why had he? Another sign that he was coming back to life?

Megan followed them through the bottom level of the town house past a laundry room, full bath and spare bedroom. A door led out into the garage and she joined the other two.

"What supplies are we gettin'?" Bayleigh asked.

Simon opened the garage door to let in light. "We need an ice chest."

"To keep the ham and cheese in?" the little girl wanted to know.

"Yes," he answered. "I thought we could put some bread on some of it in case we get hungry. And we'll keep some drinks cold."

"I like juice boxes," Bayleigh informed him.

"Somehow I thought you would."

Megan saw the flash of pain in his eyes and wondered if this whole thing was a good idea. She couldn't imagine how much he must be hurting, being around a child again. Tears burned her eyes as a lump the size of the Channel Islands formed in her throat.

"Okay," he said, letting out a long breath. "We've got work to do. I'm glad you reminded me Thanksgiving is this week. We need to catch some fish for dinner."

Bayleigh giggled. "You don't have fish on Thanksgiving. You have turkey."

"Really?" he asked, in mock surprise. "The pilgrims didn't serve fish?"

The little girl shook her head. "Nope. Turkey. My grammy's fixin' one for us."

"You're a lucky girl." He rubbed his hands together. "But the fish are waiting."

Bayleigh nodded. "I'm going to look around for supplies."

"Good idea," he agreed.

Megan watched him reach up for the ice chest resting on top of an upright freezer. In his worn jeans and plaid flannel shirt, he looked fit, fine and oh so tempting. Before she had time to carry that thought too far, he set the chest on the cement floor.

Meeting her gaze, he said, "You're uncharacteristically quiet. Something bothering you?"

"No," she lied. "I was just wondering how you're feeling. Looks like you're moving around pretty well." She studied his face. "I don't think you're going to have any scarring."

"Too bad. Chicks love scars."

She couldn't help smiling. "Yeah. So you said. I'm just wondering on what you base this observation. Personal experience?"

Why did that thought make her want to choke someone? Surely she wasn't jealous? How stupid would that be?

He rested his hands on lean hips. "Let me ask you a question. Do you, as in women in general, not have a thing for Harrison Ford?"

"Does the word *duh* mean anything to you?" When he grinned, her knees felt as if she'd just run five miles in the sand.

"Does he or does he not have a scar on his chin?"

"He does."

"I rest my case."

"Okay. But I didn't really mean the scars on your face when I inquired about your well-being. How's the leg?"

"It feels pretty good. A little stiff and sore. I actually went to see the doc."

"You're joking." Her eyes widened. Then she glanced at Bayleigh, who was poking around in a plastic container and pulling out what looked like sand toys. Apparently the little girl was too caught up in her exploration to be interested in the adults.

"Nope," he said. "I went to an orthopedic specialist, and he's got me on a regimen of physical therapy. Said the leg will be as good as new."

This was big. A major step forward. He'd signed himself out of the hospital against medical advice just a couple weeks ago. Now he'd voluntarily seen a specialist for further treatment. Megan had been listing the signs that he was ready to hear the truth. And here was one more. She should tell him.

She glanced over her shoulder at Bayleigh, who was now poking through a small storage shed standing in the corner of the garage, the part not occupied by his BMW. Now was not a good time for that discussion. It was going to be difficult for him to hear what she had to say, and she needed to do it when she and Simon were alone. Soon.

"Look what I found. It's a fishing pole just my size." Bayleigh beamed at them as she held up the treasure she'd found.

Megan's heart dropped to her toes. It had to be his son's. She rushed over to her daughter. "Bayleigh, put that down. You shouldn't touch things without asking."

She'd been afraid of this. An awkward moment with Bayleigh involved. She couldn't understand that she was a painful reminder of what Simon had lost. Megan could kick herself for agreeing to this outing. For Bayleigh—and Simon.

"But, Mommy, it's just my size. Why does Simon have one my size if I can't touch it?"

Simon stood beside them and looked down at Bayleigh. "It belonged to my son, Marcus."

"Where is he? Did he ever catch a fish with his fishin' pole?"

"Bayleigh, you shouldn't ask—"

He met her gaze and shook his head slightly. "It's all right."

He closed his eyes for a moment, then he swallowed hard. When he looked at her again, she could almost feel his pain. But then, amazingly, he smiled down at her child.

"Bayleigh, Marcus never caught a fish. I bought him that fishing pole, but he died in a car accident before he got a chance to use it."

Megan had discussed the issue of death with her daughter after a goldfish had passed on. She knew Bay knew it meant Marcus wasn't coming back.

The little girl moved beside him and slipped her little hand into his big one. "I'm sorry, Simon." Then her eyes went wide, and she clapped her other hand over her mouth. "I wasn't s'posed to say that. You're not goin' on the freeway without a car now, are you?"

To Megan's immense relief, he laughed. Squatting down in front of Bayleigh, he tapped her nose. "No. I won't go skateboarding on the freeway."

Bay breathed a sigh of relief. "I'm glad."

Impulsively she put her arms around his neck and gave him a hug. Megan held her breath for both of them. Her daughter's spontaneous show of affection could be too much for him to handle. And if he rebuffed it, Bayleigh's little heart could be deeply wounded.

Slowly Simon lifted his arms and folded the child's body against him to return the hug. "Thanks, Bayleigh, I needed that."

The little girl backed out of his arms. "Do you think

Marcus would mind if I used his fishin' pole? I promise not to break it.''

Simon smiled. ''I don't think he'd mind at all.''

''Ya-ay,'' she said. ''Can I go get the cheese and ham?''

He nodded. ''It's in the refrigerator. We're right behind you.''

After she disappeared up the stairs, Megan released a long breath. ''I don't know what to say. If I'd known—''

He pressed a gentle finger against her lips to silence her. ''No more sorrys. Simon says.''

Then he pulled her into his arms, and she knew he planned to kiss her. Every warning about this man went instantly out of her head; the worst was happening. She was in serious danger of falling for Simon Reynolds.

There was a clatter of footsteps on the stairs and a childish voice said, ''I can't find the cheese.''

''I'll go help her.'' Megan tried to pull away, but he held on to her, gently but firmly.

''You can run, but you can't hide. Not forever. If anyone knows, it's me.''

This wasn't the time to tell him he had no idea how right he was.

Chapter Thirteen

When Megan opened her door in response to his knock, Simon knew she'd been baking. She had streaks of flour on her face, smudges on her black turtleneck and white trails down the front of her soft, worn jeans where she'd rubbed her hands. The fact that Thanksgiving was the next day was also a big clue. Looking at her, he couldn't help thinking he had a lot to be thankful for this year.

"Hi," she said, obviously surprised to see him. "What are you doing here?"

"Good question," he answered, sticking his hands in his pockets. "Would you believe the town house felt too big?"

Her eyes widened. "No way."

"I missed your cooking and couldn't stomach take-out?"

"Not buying it." She folded her arms over her chest as she huffed a strand of hair out of her eyes.

It had only been a couple of days since he'd seen her. She didn't have on a speck of makeup. Her hair was tumbling out of the ponytail on top of her head. But that sweet, slender body was pretty hard to conceal, even in old jeans. She looked awfully damn cute to him. And he was like metal filings to a magnet.

"How about I got some good news and had no one to share it with?" he said.

"Now you're talking." She stepped back and held the door wide. "That one got my attention. Come on in."

It was the polite response, but uttered with the most intriguing combination of warmth and hesitation. Megan Brightwell was a very complicated woman. She fascinated the hell out of him. *That's* why he was here. But if he'd told her that she wouldn't have invited him in. And he wanted to come in. For all the reasons he'd given her.

If she and Bayleigh had never been to his place, he wouldn't have noticed how big and quiet the town house was. But they had been there, and he felt the emptiness they had left in their wake.

"Simon!" Bayleigh looked up from her place on a chair at the dinette. She jumped down and ran to him.

He opened his arms and braced himself for impact. When she reached him, he grabbed her and lifted her into his arms.

"How are you, sunshine?"

"I'm fine. Mommy and me are baking pies to take to Grammy's for Thanksgiving. Want to help?" She rested her hand trustingly on his shoulder as they looked eye to eye.

"Bay, Simon may have things to do," Megan said, leaning against the door after shutting it.

"No." He shook his head, savoring the weight and

warmth of the little girl in his arms. "Nothing pressing. What kind of pies are you making?"

"Pumpkin. Apple. And—" She wrinkled her nose as she thought. "What's that other one?"

"Mincemeat."

"I can never 'member that one," she said with a sigh. "You should come to Grammy's house with us tomorrow."

"Oh, Bay, he probably has plans," Megan said, standing up straight.

"No. But I wouldn't want to intrude."

"What's that?" the child asked.

"It's when you come over without an invitation," Megan said wryly as she met his gaze.

"I can invite him." Bayleigh looked from her mother to him. "Grammy won't mind. She always says—I forget. Something about merry."

"The more the merrier?" he suggested.

"That's it." The little girl nodded enthusiastically. "Grammy always says I can invite my friends over. Simon's my friend."

"But Grammy wasn't talking about Thanksgiving, sweetie. It's different."

"How?" The child wanted to know.

"Setting another place at the table. Last-minute guest." Megan looked at him and put her hands on her hips. "You're loving this, aren't you?"

He shrugged. "Yeah."

"I'm gonna call Grammy." She wiggled to be let down, and Simon set her on her feet.

After she raced out of the room, he asked, "Does she know the number?"

"I should let you think she's a gifted and talented child, but no. My mom is number one on the speed dial."

"She is gifted and talented," he said.

"I think she's pretty special," Megan agreed. "Look, Simon, I don't mean to sound as if you're not welcome for dinner. If I were cooking—"

He looked around. "There wouldn't be room for everyone?"

"There is that. But no. It's just—"

"You don't want me there?" He saw the truth of his question in her eyes and something else that he recognized because he felt it, too. A hungry yearning. "Or you want me there too much?"

Her expression of surprise confirmed his suspicions. But before she could weasel out of answering, the little girl ran back into the room.

"Grammy says he's more than welcome to come." Bayleigh stopped beside him and slid her small hand into his. "So are you going to?"

He knew he should let Megan off the hook, but he just couldn't bring himself to do it. And he wouldn't have to make up a lie for Janet about why he couldn't spend the holiday with her and her friends or with his folks in Phoenix. He'd be where he most wanted to be.

"I'd love to spend Thanksgiving with—" He'd started to say my two favorite girls. But that was a can of worms he didn't want to open. One step at a time. "Your family," he finished.

"Ya-ay," the little girl said as she jumped up and down.

Megan was just as easy to read. Pleasure and panic mixed together in her expression and body language. If only he could make her see she wouldn't be sorry. He wouldn't be making an effort to be her friend if he wasn't prepared to be around when she needed him.

She folded her arms over her chest. "Okay. Now that's

settled. What's the good news you stopped by to share? Let's have it.''

Then make like a tree and leave. That was the subtext of her words, Simon thought. She was definitely trying to keep her distance. She didn't know it, but he didn't plan to allow too much space between them. If he intended to cave on that, he wouldn't have accepted an invitation to holiday dinner. She'd made him feel again. And, by God, even if he wanted to, he couldn't stop now. He remembered the yearning he'd seen in her eyes when he'd pulled her into his arms the other day. She didn't really want her own space any more than he did.

Still, he couldn't shake the feeling that somehow her reluctance was about protecting Bayleigh. He'd have thought his parental radar stopped working after Marcus died. But all of a sudden it was telling him that Megan felt she had to keep him at arm's length to keep her child from harm. If she didn't know by now he wasn't like the jerk who'd walked out, he intended to show her. He wouldn't do anything to hurt her or Bayleigh.

The little girl pulled on his hand to get his attention. ''What's good news?''

Her glasses had slipped and he pushed them more firmly on her small, turned-up nose. ''Good news is something good that happened to me.''

''What happened?'' the two of them said together.

Besides meeting Megan? And this little girl? ''I got a job.''

Bayleigh jumped up and down beside him. ''Ya-ay. You won't have to live in a box under the freeway.''

He grinned. Apparently, at five, she didn't understand the concept of stocks, bonds, investments and savings. If one didn't earn a regular paycheck, one was homeless. Then his smile faded as he realized her outlook underscored how tough things had been for the two of them. And finances must have been tight. You and me against the world. Not anymore.

Megan moved away from the door and stood beside him. ''What kind of job?''

''The firm that bought out Reynolds Electronics has been after me from day one to work with them on one of my designs. They just got a big contract with an aerospace company and want me to consult on the project.''

''Congratulations, Simon.''

Bayleigh squirmed in his arms. Apparently details weren't important to her, just the fact that he wouldn't be homeless. He set her on her feet, and she went back to the table.

Then he looked down at Megan. ''Thanks.''

''It's about time you stopped wallowing in self-pity and did something productive. Something besides keeping emergency rooms in business. Gainful employment is always a good thing.''

''Ouch. Have I been that bad?''

''In a word—yes.''

Her grin took the sting out of her words as surely as a topical anesthetic. But she was right. It had been a long, dark tunnel. Now he could see the light at the end. The brightness was Megan's smile.

He stuck his hands into the pockets of his leather jacket. ''So aren't you going to invite me to stay?''

''You're not subtle, are you?''

He shook his head. ''Not when I want something.''

Her eyes took on a wary, guarded look. ''As long as it's just food.''

''What if it isn't?''

''Then you've come to the wrong place.''

''Mommy. Simon. Come see what I made.''

Saved by the five-year-old. Simon watched her hurry over to Bayleigh. He realized, not for the first time, that Megan looked as good from the rear as she did from the front. Her backside, encased in softly worn—tight—jeans, was practically a work of art. Her legs were slender, shapely, and he could picture them wrapped around his waist. He looked at the two blond heads bent together over something on the table and sighed. Life had been so much simpler when he'd been in suspended animation. Not as much fun, but definitely simpler.

He joined the two of them. Bayleigh's hands were covered with flour. In front of her were several balls of dough. Megan looked up, then straightened. She brushed something off the shoulder of his jacket.

"Sorry—" She met his gaze and stopped. "You've got some fallout here."

Bayleigh looked up. "Take your jacket off, Simon. Mommy says you shouldn't wear it inside. Only outside. You're staying, aren't you?"

He looked at Megan. "Am I?"

"I guess so."

Score one for him. Make that two. He also had tomorrow to look forward to.

Megan looked at her family gathered around the dining room table and wondered: how is it possible to be giddy with happiness and as nervous as a long-tailed cat in a room full of rocking chairs all at the same time? In a word—Simon.

Her mother had set the table with the usual eclectic mix of old, weird and tacky. On the antique lace tablecloth was the centerpiece—Dan's third-grade lopsided turkey made out of folded magazine pages painted brown. On either side were weird turkey candles set in crystal holders. Then there was the coup de grace: the regurgitating turkey gravy boat; the gravy came out of a hole in the bird's mouth. This was her mother's pride and joy from the dollar store along with the matching salt and pepper shakers.

Her father sat at the head of the table ready to carve the bird. Her mother was at the foot, closest to the kitchen and ready to hop up if anyone needed anything. Cassie sat between Dan and her fiancé Kyle Stratton. Megan had Simon and Bayleigh on either side of her because the little girl had wanted to sit by Grammy. So far everyone had been cautiously cordial to Simon. He'd related the story of how they met in the ER, which explained the almost faded but still visible marks on his face and the slight limp.

It was a measure of his intestinal fortitude that he hadn't run screaming from the room when her father and brother had grilled him after shaking his hand. Following introductions, Cassie and her mother had grinned like idiots, pointed to Simon and given her clandestine thumbs-up too many times to count.

Megan had warned them all not to mention Bayleigh's eye surgery and why. But there was always the possibility someone would forget and bring up the subject. This wasn't the way she wanted Simon to find out. But she hadn't known how to diplomatically uninvite him. Now that he was here, there was something far too right about the way he fit in with her family.

When everyone had filled their plates with turkey, dressing, mashed potatoes, cranberry salad, green bean casserole and yams the clinking and scraping in the room stopped. Everyone was quiet for several moments while her father said grace.

Then Bayleigh piped up with the dreaded words.

"Grammy, when do we get to say what we're thankful for?"

"Right now, sweet pea. Who wants to go first?"

Cassie raised her hand. She and Megan were often mistaken for twins with their similar blue eyes and blond hair. That and the fact that her sister was barely two years older.

Cass looked at the handsome brown-haired, dark-eyed man beside her. "I'm thankful for Kyle's mother."

He met her gaze. "I'm shocked and appalled. And wounded to the quick, I might add. That doesn't do a whole lot for a guy's ego."

Cassie leaned her head against his shoulder. "If she hadn't sent you to the beach the same time I was there, we wouldn't have found each other."

Kyle nodded in agreement, then leaned over and kissed her lightly, sweetly. "Okay. Then I'm thankful for my mother, too."

"Since they started," Dan chimed in, "I'll just keep it going this way. I'm thankful for bachelorhood. Ow," he said when Cassie elbowed him in the ribs.

"Easy, children," her father said. Dr. John Brightwell lifted his crystal wineglass to his wife, Mary. "I'm thankful he doesn't have a date. The family fits perfectly around the table. So go forth and stay single, son."

"Reverse psychology never worked on me, Dad."

"Okay. Can't blame me for trying." Her father looked down the length of the table and smiled at her mother. "Then I'm changing mine. I'm thankful Mary Brightwell said yes. Thirty-five years ago she took me on and there's not a day since I haven't been grateful that she did."

A resounding chorus of "awws" filled the dining room. Then her father looked at Simon. "How about you, son? I know we're an intimidating lot. But speak up."

''Yes, sir. I'm thankful for bossy new friends,'' he said.

Heat filled Megan's cheeks when he looked at her because she knew her whole family was watching her—and wondering. Her heart pounded, and she would swear her face said, *Simon and I did the wild thing.*

She cleared her throat. ''Okay. I guess it's to me. I'm thankful for all of you.''

''Mommy, you say that every year,'' Bayleigh said.

She shrugged. ''It's the truth. You're always there for me. And I don't know what I'd do without you.''

Another chorus of ''awws'' went up. Now it was time for the unpredictable child. Megan looked at her daughter. ''Your turn, pumpkin.''

Deep in thought, Bayleigh pushed her glasses up on her nose as she nudged her already cut-up turkey around her plate. ''Okay. I'm thankful Simon has a job.''

At that moment, Megan wasn't sure whether she was relieved her child hadn't mentioned her eyesight or if she wanted to wring said child's neck. She definitely wished the Brightwells were looking at her instead of Simon. At that moment something scratched at the edges of her consciousness, some momentous realization she couldn't think about now. Instinct told her she wouldn't want to think about it later, either, because it was all about the depth of her feelings for the man beside her. Glancing at him, she was astonished that he seemed unconcerned.

''Is this a recent change in economic circumstances?'' Dan asked, suspicion warring with disapproval in his tone.

''Yes,'' Simon answered. ''This turkey is delicious, Mrs. Brightwell.''

''Thank you, dear. I guess it's my turn,'' she said. ''I'm thankful that—''

''So if it's a recent job offer,'' Dan interrupted, ''are you financially—''

''Secure?'' Simon asked. ''I would say so.''

''Uncle Dan, Simon put money in the bank so he could go fishin'.''

''Your new job is fishing?'' Dan asked, disbelieving.

Megan clenched her jaw. Don't defend him. He's a big boy. He can take care of himself. Just keep your mouth shut.

''He's a consultant to the company that bought out his business,'' she blurted. ''So back off, Brightwell.''

''Interesting,'' her brother said.

''That goes double for me,'' her mother said.

''You go, girl,'' Cassie said.

''That's my girl,'' her father added.

Simon leaned over and whispered in her ear, ''Do you have any idea how turned-on I am right now?''

Megan stared at him as heat crawled up her neck and settled in her cheeks. Before she could figure out an appropriate response suitable for all genders and age groups present, her brother cleared his throat.

''So what kind of company?'' Dan asked.

''Engineering. Widgets and gizmos for airplanes. They won a contract to make whatchamacallits for the space station.'' He shrugged and forked dressing and gravy into his mouth. After chewing for several moments, he said, ''They've been after me to consult since I sold it.''

''How long ago was that?'' Kyle asked, typical nosey lawyer that he was.

''Two years.''

''How come you didn't take them up on the offer then?'' Cassie wanted to know. Typical nosy sister—a perfect match for the inquisitive lawyer.

''I needed—''

"Time off," Megan finished for him. "Now, if you guys are finished with the third degree—"

"Hey, kidlet," Dan said to his niece. "What's all this about fishing?"

"Mommy and I went with Simon. He has a house by the ocean. And he has a fishin' pole my size. He let me use it because his little boy never got to."

Uh-oh. There it was. Leave it to Bayleigh to put the elephant right there on the table. Now Megan had to figure out what to do about it.

Simon smiled at Bayleigh, then looked at the rest of her family, who all seemed frozen. "Marcus, my son, was killed in an auto accident two years ago. Along with his mother, my ex-wife."

Cassie gasped, but that was the only sound in the room. Megan held her breath, but no one said they were sorry. God bless the Brightwells.

Finally, her brother said, "No wonder you needed time off."

"Simon?" Bayleigh said.

"Hmm?" he asked, looking down at her.

"Do you think Marcus would mind that I used his fishin' pole? Even if I didn't catch any fish?"

Leave it to the five-year-old to cut to the guts of the matter. Megan held her breath.

Simon looked past her to the little girl and the corners of his mouth turned up. A tender expression slipped into his eyes, and it tugged at Megan's heart.

"Bayleigh, I think Marcus would be very happy to share with you."

"I'm glad." The little girl smiled as if a great weight was lifted from her shoulders.

Megan's mother raised her wineglass. "We're thankful to have you with us for the holiday this year, Simon."

Along with everyone else, Simon raised his glass. "Thank you. It's nice to be had."

"So, kidlet, Simon took you fishing," Dan said, when everyone stopped laughing. "I was going to do that. I'm hurt that you went out with another man."

"You always have to work," Bayleigh said in a scolding tone that Megan was afraid sounded very much like her own.

"You noticed that, huh?" Dan said.

"She's smart, Dan. She notices everything and takes no prisoners," Megan pointed out.

"Like her mother," Simon met her gaze.

"Well," Mary Brightwell said, "I don't believe I've said what I'm thankful for."

"Grammy, you're thankful Simon is here."

"That thankful was for all of us, dear. I get to have one just for me. And I've got just the one. I'm thankful that Cassie and Kyle are getting married."

"Me, too." Cassie looked at Kyle and grinned. "I've decided one of the marriage perks is not wondering whether or not I'll have a date on Saturday nights."

Dan made a dismissive noise. "I might not have a Thanksgiving date, but I've got one for your wedding."

"Who?" Bayleigh wanted to know.

"Your mom." He lifted his chin in Megan's direction. "She's the MOH—maid of honor, and I'm the best man. We get to walk down the aisle together."

"I don't have a date," Bayleigh said, and pouted.

"You can be mine," her grandfather offered.

"No, I can't. You're Grammy's date."

The older man smiled at his wife. "Can't argue with that. But I could have two dates."

"I want my own," the little girl said.

"But you're the flower girl," Megan reminded her. "What about the ring bearer?"

"There's not going to be one," Cassie said. "None of our friends have a son the right age. Dan's going to do double duty."

"See?" Bayleigh complained. "I don't have anyone to walk with."

"You can bring a guest," Kyle offered. He was such a softie where the little girl was concerned. "Why don't you ask someone?"

"Do you know anyone in kindergarten who has a driver's license?" Dan teased.

"You're silly, Uncle Dan," she scoffed. After chewing thoughtfully for several moments, she said, "Simon can drive. He brought mommy and me here in his car."

Uh-oh, Megan thought. Everyone at this table would have to be deaf, dumb and blind not to see where this was headed. But surely after holiday dinner, Simon would have had a bellyful of the Brightwells. He would probably have a convenient excuse. He had to. She was afraid too much togetherness could result in an acute case of Simonitis—inflammation of her heart caused by prolonged exposure to Simon Reynolds.

"Simon?" the little girl said.

"Hmm?"

"Would you go with me to Aunt Cassie and Uncle Kyle's wedding?"

"It would be my pleasure to escort such a lovely young lady."

Megan groaned inwardly when the child smiled happily. But the event was two weeks and two days off. Not only was that enough time for him to back out, it was a little over fourteen days in which to fortify herself against the attraction to him that just wouldn't quit.

"Why did you decide to have the wedding in December?" Simon asked.

Cassie looked at her fiancé. "Tell him, Mr. Romance."

"We wanted to get married before the end of the year so we could file joint income tax." Kyle grinned.

"Smooth," Simon said wryly.

"No kidding. And what's this *we* stuff?" Cassie demanded. "It was your idea."

"Would you believe," Kyle said seriously, "that I wanted to start out the new year with you by my side—physically, emotionally, legally?"

"Okay," Cassie agreed happily. "That works."

"Right after Aunt Cassie gets married, we're havin' a play at school." Bayleigh squirmed on her chair. A sure sign she'd been sitting too long.

"I thought you were a pilgrim yesterday," Simon commented.

"I was, but we just wore hats we made out of construction paper."

"Do you have a part in the play, Bayleigh?" her grandmother asked.

The little girl nodded. "I'm going to be an angel."

"Typecasting," Simon murmured.

"I get to wear a costume and everything. I need wings and a halo and a white dress."

"This is the first I've heard about it," Megan said, a knot forming in her stomach. So much for being an experienced kindergarten parent. "Where are we going to get that stuff?"

"I can whip up a simple white dress," her mother said.

"But what about the other things?" Megan asked. "I've never been especially crafty."

"Yeah," Cassie piped up. "Remember when she insisted on taking that shop class in high school? Because she liked Mike Hawkins—'' Her sister stopped when she saw the glare Megan was shooting her. ''Anyway, who can forget that wooden bowl she made.''

''The one with the hole in the bottom,'' Dan said laughing. ''And the mirror. Do you still have it? Remember the gouges around the outside? You took a hunk out of it smoothing the wrong way and had to try and even it all the way around.''

''Thanks, you guys,'' she said. ''I appreciate the stroll down memory lane detailing the stellar exploits of shop class. But it wasn't especially helpful.''

''I can help,'' Dan said.

''You have to work,'' Bayleigh said, looking worried.

''She's got your number, Dan.'' Megan met his gaze across the table.

''What are we going to do if you can't make the rest of my costume, Mommy?''

Simon rested his fork on his empty plate. ''Maybe I can help.''

She knew he was crafty. After all, he was here with her family against her better judgment. But was he good with his hands? She knew the answer to that too because the memory of his touch sent a shiver through her. But most important, she didn't want her daughter to be embarrassed in front of the whole school.

''I don't know, Simon. Do you know how?''

''I think I can manage.'' He sent her a wry look. ''I'm an engineer.''

''He makes airplanes, Mommy.''

''Parts,'' he clarified. ''But wings are parts.''

Bayleigh slipped off her chair and stood next to him. ''Can you make me some really cool ones? Hannah said her daddy is making really cool ones, and I want some, too.''

Simon looked at Megan and his expression told her he wanted to say yes. But she had to speak now or forever hold her peace. When she saw the hopeful, earnest look on her daughter's little face, she held her peace. Besides, she wanted Bayleigh to be the best-looking angel ever. An engineer would come in handy. How could she say no?

"I promise you'll have the coolest wings in kindergarten," he finally said.

"Really?" Bayleigh's eyes grew big and round and excited. "And will you come to my play?"

"I wouldn't miss it for anything. But we'll have to start on those wings right away."

And that was how Megan's two-week and two-day window slammed shut. And boy could she have used that time.

A holiday dinner with the Brightwells had been an eye-opener. From the moment she'd walked in the door with Simon, her instinct to protect and defend him had instantly switched on. That meant only one thing: she cared about him. More than nurse for patient. More than friends.

More than she wanted to.

Chapter Fourteen

"I think more sparkles." Bayleigh inspected the angel's wings Simon had just finished constructing.

Megan's kitchen table looked like a craft store had exploded all over it. Bits of white netting, ribbon, glitter and glue cluttered the newspapers she'd spread out to protect the furniture.

She'd just bathed Bayleigh and the child smelled of soap, shampoo and sleepy little girl. Her still-wet hair had grooves where her mother had run a brush through it. The familiar scents unlocked thoughts of Marcus, and Simon waited for the pain that always sucked the breath out of him. When it didn't happen, he was unsettled. Sad but not destroyed. He would always miss his son. But he felt ready now to remember, and it was okay to let the memories make him smile.

Thanks to Megan. And her little girl.

If not for Bayleigh, he'd have had to find another excuse to hang out with her mom.

"More glitter?" He studied the angel's wings fashioned from wire, an overlay of netting, bits of ribbon and the small but nearly empty bottle of silver sparkles. "This is just my opinion, Bayleigh, but if you put any more glittery stuff on, they're going to have to hand out sunglasses to the audience."

"That's silly, Simon." She grinned at his exaggeration. "Mommy, what do you think?"

Megan put her arm around the little girl, who retreated to the other side of the table and nestled beside her. "I hate being the tie-breaker."

"It builds character," Simon pointed out. "Parenthood isn't for the faint of heart. Honesty is the best policy. And that means no taking sides based on family connections. Nepotism is pretty unattractive."

She leveled him with a droll look. "If you wanted to do this your way, why didn't you just say so? What did you need us for?"

Good question. On the one hand, he fought the urge to camp out on her doorstep just to see her and monopolize every free moment she had. On the other, he didn't want to be interested in Megan Brightwell. Fate had a way of making you pay when you cared too much.

But he'd promised himself to show her not all guys leave. So here he was making angel wings. As promised. For the angel who had grabbed him by the lapels and yanked him kicking and screaming out of perpetual midnight. Since she had, he was going to try to return the favor.

On Thanksgiving he'd sensed her reluctance to have him involved in her life—not to mention this school project and her sister's wedding. He could almost see that she was holding back, forcing herself to deny the attraction arcing between them. She could lay down rules all she wanted, but it was so much wasted breath. Sooner or later he and Megan were going up in flames.

"Simon? Are you okay?" Bayleigh peered at him through her glasses.

"Hmm? Yeah. I'm fine." For the first time in a long time, he was telling the truth. He *was* okay. "What was the question?"

Megan's eyes narrowed as she studied him. "I bet you didn't play well with others when you were growing up."

"What does that mean?"

"If you didn't want input on wing construction, why did you include us in the project?"

He met her gaze as he thought about the question. "A couple reasons, I guess. First, it's Bayleigh's play, and she has to wear the costume. It's fun. And I forgot how much I missed…kids."

He'd been about to say family, but the shadows in Megan's eyes stopped him. "So what do you think? To glitter or not to glitter? That's the question."

Megan tapped her lips as she studied the wings. "More isn't necessarily better. Sometimes less is more. On the other hand, we're going to lose some in transport."

"You said your mom sewed the dress part. Maybe we should attach these and have Bayleigh try it on. See how it looks. Under the lights."

The little girl shook her head. "It's bad luck."

Megan looked at her. "Where did you hear that?"

"At Grammy's on Thanksgiving. Uncle Kyle was trying to get Aunt Cassie to let him see her wedding dress. She said it was bad luck for him to see it before the big day."

"That's just a wedding superstition, sweetie," Megan

explained. "It has nothing to do with costumes for kindergarten plays. Why don't you try it on so we can see how it looks?"

Stubbornly she shook her head. "Nope."

"I guess you're just going to have to wait until the big day to see the fruits of your labor." Then her smile disappeared. "That is, I'll take lots of pictures. I didn't mean to imply that you had to come to the performance."

"But you *are* going to be there, Simon. You said you would." Bayleigh stifled a yawn.

"Simon's working now, sweetie. Maybe he doesn't have time to take off during the day for the play."

"Can you?"

He smiled. "That's the nice thing about being a consultant. I tell them what time I can consult. I'll be there."

"Promise?"

"Count on it," he said fervently.

"Bay, it's bedtime now. Say good-night to Simon."

"Do I hafta, Mommy? Just five more minutes?" When her mother shook her head, she said, "Four? Three? Two?"

"Zero. Let's go. Say good-night."

"Oka-ay." The little girl could have moved slower as she rounded the table, but she would have come to a stop. Then she put her arms up for a hug. "'Night, Simon."

Simon resisted the tug on his heart for just a moment before folding her small body into his arms. "Sleep tight, kiddo."

Megan hustled her down the hallway and the murmur of voices drifted to him. For the second time that night he felt contentment slip over him. Is this what living again was like? People to care about. To count on him. To come home to. A special woman to laugh with. Love with.

Almost before he had a chance to miss her, Megan was back. She folded her arms over her chest as she surveyed the mess on the table. When she met his gaze, her mouth turned up at the corners.

"I bet your employees were glad when you sold the company."

Surprised at her observation, he asked, "Why would you think that?"

"You're a slave driver. Bayleigh's head hardly hit the pillow before she was asleep."

He laughed. "She's something else. And let's talk about who wore out whom."

"Good point. She's definitely a bundle of energy."

He picked up the newly constructed wings and turned them to the light to inspect the handiwork. "Don't sugar-coat it now. Tell me what you really think. More glitter?"

She shook her head. "The fashion police wouldn't let her into heaven..." She stopped as if she'd inadvertently revealed a national security secret. "Simon, I didn't mean to bring up—I mean that was thoughtless. To spoil your mood—"

"No. It's a relief. I've held things in too long. There's no need to censor yourself. In fact, I've been thinking about Marcus a lot tonight." If he didn't know better, he would call the look on her face guilty. But that was ridiculous. She'd made him see holding back was a waste of time and energy. "It feels good to remember him. Less pain than I thought there'd be. Just good memories. Did I tell you he was about Bayleigh's age when I lost him. I wonder if he would have been in a Christmas play in kindergarten?"

"Simon—" Megan moved closer and stood beside him. Close enough for him to feel the warmth of her body, smell the scent of her skin through her matching black fleece pants and shirt. She looked at him until he met her gaze.

"What?"

"Bayleigh can't take his place."

"I know." He sighed. "That's not what this is about. I'm not doing that. Believe me. It's just that she's so...busy. Talking. Observing. She has her own five-year-old take on the world."

"If she's too much just say so—"

"No. Never. I've had enough quiet to last the rest of my life. I'm not looking for her to replace Marcus. No one could do that. It's just—" He ran his fingers through his hair. "I'm a selfish bastard, but this is the truth. I miss him a little less when I build angel wings with her. Or escort her to a wedding." He slipped an arm around her waist and urged her onto his lap. "Don't you feel it, too?"

"Feel what?"

"Less lonely."

"But I'm not. I've got my work, my child, my family—"

"Is that enough?"

"Yes. I'm fine."

He tightened his grip when she started to push herself away. "Are you? Then why do you keep your distance?"

"I told you why, the first time we met and played nurse and the daredevil."

"I remember. And it's only fair to warn you I'm determined to prove you wrong. Any resemblance to *him* is entirely fabricated by you to keep me at a distance."

"Don't, Simon—"

"What?"

"We can't have a future even if I wanted one."

''If you're going to give Bayleigh a traditional family with a mother *and* a father, sooner or later you're going to have to let your guard down.''

Refusing to put her arm around him, she clasped her fingers together in her lap. ''I don't know if I can. But that's not why you and I don't stand a chance.''

''Then why?'' Until that moment, he would have sworn he didn't even want a chance. But now...

''I have something to tell you.'' She looked at him, studying, taking his measure, gauging...what? His strength? He was doing fine physically. And what did that have to do with anything?

''Okay. Let's have it.''

''It's about Bayleigh's eyesight.'' She slipped off his lap and started cleaning up the table.

''What about it?''

''The surgery—'' She turned, her hands clutching bits of scraps from the project until her knuckles turned as white as the netting. ''I don't know how—it's hard to say—''

''Just spit it out.''

She sighed and looked away. ''There are no guarantees. Her vision is fine now. But any time she could—''

He stood behind her and rubbed his hands up and down her arms. ''No one knows better than me that life doesn't come with a guarantee. If you're trying to scare me away, it's not going to work. I'm not going anywhere.''

''You can't be sure. I don't want you to make promises to her that you can't keep.''

''And what about you?'' He turned her toward him.

Doubt swirled in her eyes. ''I learned not to count on anyone.''

''Is that what you wanted to tell me?''

"Pretty much," she said, then turned away and started stuffing scraps of stuff from the table into a plastic bag.

As badly as he wanted to pull her back into his arms and kiss her, he sensed it was the worst thing he could do. Something was bothering her and she wasn't ready to talk yet. He knew her well enough not to push her further away by getting too personal before she was ready. So he helped her pick up the trash. After all, isn't that what life was about? Picking up the pieces and moving on?

Because as much as he didn't want to care deeply again, she'd made him realize it wasn't always about what he wanted. It's about what was. Megan had come in under his radar. Before he knew it, he'd started to need her. But she was trying to ignore the fact that she needed him, too. He would make her see you couldn't bury your head in the sand without leaving your backside exposed.

Sitting at the head table, Megan watched her married sister and new brother-in-law dance. Wedding vows had gone off without a hitch. The reception was winding down now, but it had been perfect. Location, location, location. The Odyssey Restaurant was high on a hill overlooking the spectacular twinkling lights of the San Fernando Valley. The large banquet room looked like a fairyland with flowers, small white lights and candles.

Simon was beside her looking more handsome than she'd ever seen him in a charcoal suit with gray shirt and matching satin tie.

He looked at her and smiled. "Have I told you how beautiful you look tonight?"

"As a matter of fact—no. But I'm sure it's the dress." The spaghetti strap, cream satin dress with chiffon overlay and pink rosebuds appliquéd on the scalloped bodice made her *feel* beautiful. Her daughter was wearing the little-girl version with little cream-colored bows at the straps. "Do I look as good as your date?"

He glanced across the room where Bayleigh was with several children. One was a boy of ten she'd been shadowing since the reception started. "My date dumped me." The feigned hurt on his face made her laugh. "I'm drowning my sorrows."

"I happen to know for a fact you're drinking ginger ale." He shrugged, drawing her attention to the width of his shoulders in the expensive jacket. If only he looked like a troll, she thought.

"To each his own when dealing with a broken heart."

"Imagine her spurning you for a blond, blue-eyed god closer to her own age. She's just like my sister."

"How's that?"

Megan's glance slid to Cassie and Kyle, smiling, dancing, kissing, generally being in love. How she envied the happiness they shared. How she longed for the same thing. If only the first man to make her think about it wasn't the wrong man.

She met his gaze again and sighed. "Cassie fell in love with Kyle when she was a kid and has spent the past twenty-five years getting her man. Tyler—"

"The blue-eyed god?"

"The very one. He lives next door to my folks. Bayleigh plays at his house with his younger sister."

Simon watched the children and a wary expression slipped into his eyes. "If he so much as touches a single bow on her pretty little dress, I'll squash him like a bug."

"Even though she dumped you?"

He looked at her and smiled wryly. "Yup."

"Spoken like a true—"

"Yes?"

Father. She'd been about to say it because that's the way he'd been acting. "Spoken like a jealous suitor," she said instead. She forced a lightness into her tone that was a complete lie.

Because it's what she *hadn't* said that was torturing her. She should have told him the truth up front. She should have told him of the bond their children shared. It would have been so much easier before...before what? Before her emotions had become engaged? Before her child had met him? He'd come over almost every evening since Thanksgiving two weeks ago. Bay was becoming attached. If Simon's behavior was any indication, he was forming an attachment of his own. But she'd listened to Janet and waited.

"Instead of drowning my sorrows in ginger ale, how about dancing with me to help me forget?"

The invitation, innocently offered, sparked a sexual awareness that shot straight to her abdomen and a rhythmic throbbing between her legs. Dance with him? Have his arms around her? Be close to his body?

"I'd love to," she said.

They stood at the same time and he slid her chair back, then took her hand and led her onto the dance floor in the center of the room. He put his hand at her waist and drew her against him, then wrapped her other hand in his palm and rested the two on his chest. The closeness with him was like coming home. Why did he have to be the one to make her heart beat faster? The only one who twisted, tangled and turned her senses inside out and upside down? Fate had a lousy sense of humor. She was the one who had to tell him about his son.

The night he'd made the angel wings, she'd had the perfect opportunity but couldn't make the words come out of her mouth. When he found out about Bayleigh's transplant, he would turn his back. He'd never approved the decision to donate his son's organs. How could he not resent the living child when he knew the truth?

Megan believed him when he'd said he wasn't trying to substitute her and Bayleigh for the family he'd lost. What he was doing was far more dangerous. He was making both of them fall in love with him. How could she resist a man who loved as deeply as Simon?

As they moved slowly around the dance floor, she heard someone say, ''Are you next down the aisle, Megan?''

In a sensuous haze, she looked around to find who'd asked the question, but whoever it was had waltzed by.

''Don't mind that,'' she said. ''You know how people at weddings are. They want to match up everyone who isn't attached.''

''I wasn't minding anything,'' he said, his voice a throaty sound that raised gooseflesh on her arms. ''Except the fact that as much as I like the way you look in this dress, I'd like you even more out of it.''

She froze as she met his gaze. A similar thought hadn't been far from her mind—not since the first time. ''But I—''

''You're not my nurse now and you haven't been for quite some time. Don't even play the impropriety card.''

''Simon, there's something I have to say—''

The music ended and her brother stood in the center of the dance floor with a microphone as the lights grew brighter. They stopped dancing, but Simon didn't let her go. He snuggled her to his side and slid his arm around her waist, tightening his grip.

''Ladies, this is the moment you've all been waiting for. Cassie is going to throw her bouquet. If all the single women will gather in the center of the floor, I'll be glad to take your phone numbers.''

''C'mon, Megan,'' Cassie said, as she walked by then stopped beside their brother.

She looked up at Simon. ''I guess I have to do this.''

''It's flowers, not a firing squad, Megan.''

''It just feels like a firing squad,'' she mumbled, reluctantly moving away from the warmth and security of his arms.

But Megan laughed in spite of herself as she joined the giggling group. Cassie stood a little apart, her full-skirted white dress billowing around her. Her veil was long gone, but a wreathlike crown of white roses and baby's breath still circled her upswept blond hair.

''Get ready, Megan,'' she whispered.

Cassie had informed her earlier that she was going to throw the bouquet in her direction. Cassie wanted to do everything possible to ensure Megan was the next bride. How pathetic was that?

''Do we have all the single ladies? Bayleigh?'' Dan asked, surveying the guests.

Megan spotted her daughter on the other side of the circle standing beside Simon. The little girl shook her head and shyly burrowed next to the tall man who put his hand on her shoulder, protectively keeping her at his side. Her heart cracked at the sight.

''Okay, then,'' Dan said. ''Cass, it's time for your Hail Mary pass.''

''Head's up, Megan,'' Cassie called and turned away.

Then the flowers went flying over the bride's shoulder. Megan caught them easily and endured the good-natured grumbling of the other single ladies. She walked over to her daughter and handed her the bouquet.

''Thanks, Mommy.''

''You're welcome.'' She met Simon's amused gaze.

Everyone gathered around laughed and clapped.

Dan came forward with the microphone. ''That's my niece.'' He cleared his throat. ''Okay, guys. It's our turn. Single men gather round. Kyle's going to remove the garter with his teeth.''

''Dan!'' Cassie protested.

But a chair appeared and she sat in it and discreetly inched up her full white skirt. Down on one knee, Kyle grinned at his really and truly blushing bride and slid the lace and ribbon circle from his wife's thigh. Whistles, cheers and catcalls accompanied his actions.

Then he stood and turned his back. The garter went sailing in Simon's direction. Imagine that. Forget divine intervention. The Brightwells took matters into their own hands. And Simon was up to the challenge. He snagged it easily, while Megan's heart broke just a little more. The other bachelors clapped him on the back.

''Mommy, I'm tired.'' Bayleigh stood beside her along with her grandparents. ''Grammy and Grampy are leaving now. Can I have a sleepover with them?''

''Sweetie, I'll take you home.'' She looked at her parents, who were standing just behind the little girl.

''Why don't you stay until the reception's over,'' her mother said.

''Don't you guys want to watch Cassie and Kyle leave?''

''No need. In the morning we're taking them to the airport for the honeymoon trip.'' Her father put his arm around his wife. ''Frankly, I'm tired, too. It would give us a good excuse to leave before I get cranky.''

''You're sure?'' she asked, looking from one to the other.

"They're sure, Mom, or they wouldn't have said so," Bayleigh pointed out.

"I guess she's heard all this before," Megan said, laughing.

"Heard what?" Simon asked, as he joined them.

"I'm taking your date and mine home," her dad said. He put his hand up when Simon started to protest. "It's all decided. You young folks stay. Knock yourselves out."

"Yes, sir."

Megan bent to give her daughter a hug and kiss. "Be good. I'll see you in the morning. Bye. Love you."

"Bye, love you, Mommy. Bye, Simon," she said, waving as she turned away.

How long would it be before the little girl tacked a "love you" onto that for Simon? Megan knew she had to tell him everything before things got any worse. She waved as the three of them threaded their way between groups of guests then disappeared through the doorway.

He held out his hand. "Isn't there some tradition that the guy who catches the garter has to dance with the woman who snagged the bouquet?"

Megan looked at the broad palm and long fingers, thinking it was more tempting than a box of chocolate-covered nuts and caramel. She wasn't up for a debate or a denial and willingly put her hand in his. "If there isn't a custom, there ought to be."

He led her onto the dance floor as the strains of a love song filled the air. Megan went into his arms even more willingly than before and sighed when he urged her snugly against him. "Thank you for making this night special for Bayleigh."

"It was my pleasure. She's special. Like her mom."

Megan's heart began to pound. Surely he could feel it

as easily as she felt the vibrations of his deep voice course through her while they moved slowly over the floor. Her breasts were pressed to his chest and she was gloriously grateful for the plunging back of her dress that allowed his palm to caress her bare skin. Heat shot straight through her like a fireball.

"Have I told you lately how beautiful you look?" His tone was low, husky, seductive and raised goose bumps all over.

"Yes, a little while ago. But I wouldn't mind hearing it again."

"The way you look tonight—" He tightened his hold on her.

"What?"

"I want to have a sleepover, too."

Startled, Megan's feet stopped moving as she looked up and met his gaze. The emotions simmering there were enough to scorch her and steal the oxygen from her lungs. "I—I don't know what to say to that."

"Your place or mine? Makes no difference to me." When she opened her mouth, he continued. "I know the rules and like I said before, they don't apply anymore. There's no reason we can't be together."

Chapter Fifteen

Megan couldn't get her apartment door unlocked, her hand was shaking so badly. Not from fear, nerves or cold. Desire poured through her. Hot, molten, breath-stealing hunger for Simon. She'd hoped the drive from the reception to her apartment would have been long enough to cool her desire. But as Simon took the keys from her hand, the smoldering look in his eyes told her a trip from here to the moon wouldn't be far enough.

"Let me," he said.

In moments, they were tucked away inside. When he slid his hands around her waist and tugged her to him, her purse slid from her shoulder and clunked to the floor. The part of her brain not consumed with Simon knew everything had fallen out and was strewn everywhere. But she didn't care.

Not when she was so desperate for him. This was selfish. But tonight could be all she would ever have with him. If she only had one night left on this earth, she wanted to spend it in Simon's arms.

He kissed her deeply, then pulled back, breathing heavily. He started to shrug out of his jacket.

"Let me," she said.

She put her palms on his chest, then slid them up toward his shoulders, pushing his coat off as she went. She loosened his tie and grabbed one end, pulling it hand over hand without taking her gaze from his. After tugging the tails of his shirt free, she started at his collar and undid the buttons one by one until his chest was bared to her curious gaze and her eager touch.

He took her wrist, lifting until he kissed each of her fingertips, then licked her palm. Her breathing escalated yet she couldn't seem to draw enough air into her lungs while shivers of need raced through her.

"Let's take this into the other room," he said, his voice hoarse with fierceness.

She couldn't have protested even if she'd wanted. And she definitely didn't want to. With her hand tucked tightly in his, he led her down the hall and into her bedroom. He flipped the switch on the lamp beside the bed, casting the room and her unmade bed into subdued light.

"I was in a hurry this morning," she explained. "What with the wedding and all."

He urged her toward the bed until the backs of her knees touched the mattress. "Tell me why you didn't want to catch the bouquet tonight."

"It implies wanting to get married." She unbuttoned the cuffs of his shirt, then slipped it off his shoulders.

"Don't you?" He leaned down, touching his lips to her neck.

She gasped at the jolt of pleasure that zinged through her. "If I did—"

"If? Not when?"

"Is this any time to psychoanalyze me?"

"It works for me. They say taking your clothes off doesn't make you vulnerable. It's expressing your feelings."

"They? Dr. Phil?"

"Whoever. I think working in the ER is safe for you because patients are in and out. Short-term. You don't have a chance to get attached."

She blinked, then stared at him. She'd never thought of it that way. "That's good."

"I can do better."

When he grinned, her insides melted like chocolate in a double boiler. "If it's all the same to you, would you stop messing with my mind and just kiss me?"

"Happy to oblige." But first he turned her around.

Megan felt his warm fingers on the zipper of her dress. Slowly he tugged it down, letting his knuckles graze her back all the way to her backside. He slipped his hands beneath the straps and gripped her upper arms as the satin slid down her body and pooled at her feet. In the next instant he'd dispensed with her strapless bra and everything else. He picked her up in his arms and deposited her gently in the center of her double bed. Then he took a foil square from his wallet and set it on her nightstand before scattering his clothes on the floor.

In the dim light, she let her gaze roam over his body—the chiseled face, wide shoulders, the sprinkling of hair over his chest tapering to a line over his flat stomach, long muscular legs. Then there was his most impressive reaction to her. It seemed an eternity before he finally lowered himself to the bed and stretched out beside her.

"Now, I'll kiss you." His voice was just this side of a growl, and he was breathing hard.

It was nice not to be the only one. And when his mouth descended to within a whisper of hers, she was glad not to be able to form a coherent thought. "For the record," she said breathlessly, "I'm a sucker for a man who takes charge."

"Good."

He nibbled her lips, then took charge of the very sensitive place just beneath her ear. He took such masterful charge she nearly shot up off the bed as intense pleasure rushed through her. But the sensations evoked by his strong hands held her in place. She couldn't suppress a small moan of delight when he cupped her breast and brushed his thumb over her nipple.

But she was pleased he wasn't completely cool in his mastery. His hand shook.

She nestled next to him, feeling the length of his maleness flex at the touch of her femininity. Moving against him, she heard his breath as he hissed through his teeth. Pleased, she reached out and guided his face back to hers, kissing him. He traced her mouth with his tongue, urging her to open. When she did, he dipped inside, stroking her until the fire in her belly burned bright and hot. Heat spread from the tips of her toes to the top of her head and the places in between.

"Simon, please," she whispered.

"Soon."

"No. Now."

He laughed and she felt the vibration where the warm skin of his chest flattened her sensitive breasts. "What Megan wants, Megan gets?"

If only that were true. Then she would get him. But she couldn't think about that now. She only wanted to feel. And remember.

He reached for the foil packet and carefully opened it,

though his hands shook. After covering himself, he kissed her hard, pressing her into the mattress with his body. Then he levered himself between her thighs and took his weight on his forearms as he settled against her. With a single forceful thrust, he was inside her.

She sighed, savoring the wonder of being one with this man. It felt right—like coming home. But it felt amazing when he started to move. Slowly at first as she searched for a rhythm, then faster when she found it. He took her on a magic carpet ride. Just when she thought she couldn't go any higher, her breath caught at the dizzying peak.

Tension built within her, up and up until the lights behind her eyes grew brighter than the fireworks on the Fourth of July. Release rippled through her—wave after wave of bone-melting satisfaction. A moment later, Simon's body tensed and froze. His arms went around her, pressing her to his chest as he groaned out his own gratification.

He was still for several moments. Then he cupped her cheek in his palm and kissed her tenderly, before rolling away. Some part of her registered the fact that the light in the bathroom went on and off before he was beside her again. He slid an arm beneath her and nestled her against him.

"Who knew six could be so mind-blowing," he said, reminding her of her hasty explanation to her daughter.

"You're going to hell." She started to giggle.

They laughed until she cried. Just one whole night in his arms. That's all she asked. Tomorrow, she would tell him everything.

Simon carefully slipped out of Megan's bed so he wouldn't wake her. He put on his pants and went into the kitchen to start coffee. Yanking open the refrigerator door, he assessed the contents, then pulled out eggs and biscuits. No breakfast meat here. No cholesterol in the veins of Megan's life.

After last night, he was pretty sure his campaign to show her he wasn't that kind of guy was working. At least he hoped so. Because he intended to be in her life for a long time. How could he not? After so long in the dark, he couldn't seem to get enough of the light. He would probably always carry a pocket of guilt inside him for what had happened to Marcus. The "if onlys" would always be there. But they wouldn't keep him from moving on.

Whistling, he went through her cupboards and found a pan and cookie sheet. He preheated the oven then set the doughy circles out for baking. After eggs were cracked and whipped in the bowl, he figured there was nothing to do but wait until the sexy sleepyhead in the other room decided to drag herself out of bed. He intended to give her a hot breakfast for a change. As hot as the love they'd made last night.

The thought made him grin as he walked through her living room on his way to the door and the daily newspaper outside it. Just on the threshold, he saw Megan's purse where she'd dropped it. Simon recalled the heat and need he'd felt and the reflection of the same in her eyes and his smile widened. His smiles came easily since meeting Megan. He knew she was more than a friend. The *L* word popped into his mind, but he wasn't ready to go there.

He squatted down, picked up her wallet, keys and sunglasses and stuffed them into her bag. A plastic expandable picture holder, halfway open, was nearby. Leave it to Megan to carry a walking photo album with her. He grabbed it and couldn't resist glancing through. Shots of Bayleigh as a baby. Her first school picture. One of her with her grandparents.

The last one startled him. A cold feeling crept over him as he recognized the woman with Bayleigh. Images flashed through his mind in a puzzled jumble. This photo was the piece that completed the picture.

He heard movement behind him, then Megan slid her arms around his waist. She was wearing a terry-cloth robe, but even through that he felt her breasts pressed to his back. Then the softness of her cheek as she rubbed against him. "Good morning."

The sunshine in her voice lasered his heart in half. The feel of her made his body respond as if it had a mind of its own. Tension coiled through him.

He knew she felt it when she lifted her head. "What is it, Simon?"

He turned and held out the picture of Janet and Bayleigh. "Were you ever going to tell me?"

Everything fell into place. Why Bayleigh's father had left. The little girl's eye problems. Corrective surgery. Janet had told him the recipient of Marcus' corneas was a little girl. She kept in touch with the child. Everything had been right in front of him, but he'd refused to see.

"Tell you what?" Megan took the pictures and saw the one he'd been looking at. "Oh, God—" She looked at him, shock and surprise swirling in her eyes. "What are the odds? Of all the emergency rooms in all the world, you had to roll into mine," she whispered. The words were light, a reference to one of the most tragic romantic movies of all time.

Appropriate, he thought, bitter anger surging through him. He rested his hands on his hips. "Don't you have anything to say? Were you ever going to clue me in?"

"Yeah. But I'm not sure you're willing to hear me."

"Try."

She sighed and walked into the kitchen. "I need coffee. Want some?"

"No."

She reached into the cupboard and pulled out a mug. He had the satisfaction of seeing that her hand was shaking.

After pouring the hot, dark liquid into her cup, she faced him. Her expression was blank, carefully blank, he thought. But her knuckles went white as she gripped the cup like a life preserver.

"I had no idea who you were when the paramedics wheeled you into the emergency room. It wasn't until that first day the home care agency sent me to you."

How could he forget? As much as he might like to. "What happened?"

"I quit."

He remembered. He'd kissed her to scare her away. And it had worked. She had left in a huff. Twenty minutes later she'd come back with some bull about doing no harm. He'd bought into it because he'd wanted to so badly. He hated that. But he'd been hurting, physically and mentally. When she'd returned, it seemed nothing hurt as bad. He hated that, too.

She took a sip of her coffee, then met his gaze. "When I walked out, I ran into Janet. She was coming back to make sure you were all right. She'd been to see you earlier and you had chased her away, too, with your scintillating personality. Mr. Congeniality."

He ignored the sarcasm, refusing to get sucked in again by her humor and spunk. But he remembered that day clearly. Janet had been to see him and left in a hurry saying she wasn't through with him. She must have returned as Megan was leaving. Until this moment, it never occurred to him to wonder why she hadn't stopped by again. Now he knew that she knew he had Megan. He sucked in a breath at the pain.

"So the two of you are in this together." When she nodded, rage rolled through him, gathering force like a tidal wave. "Whose idea was it to play me for a fool?"

She met his gaze and something flashed in her blue eyes. "It wasn't like that, Simon. She cares about you. And I—"

He held a hand up. "Don't even go there. Just tell me why you kept me in the dark."

"When we sorted out why we were both there, she was excited that you had asked for me personally to be your nurse. She said it was the first time you'd reached out, a positive sign that you were beginning to move forward, to put the accident behind you—"

"I'll never do that."

She ignored him. "I wanted to tell you I knew everything. I wanted to thank you for giving Bayleigh a chance at normal. Because of the transplant, she can get her driver's license, put on makeup, have a favorite color, see the faces of her babies one day. I had to find a way to show my gratitude for the miracle you gave my daughter."

"It wasn't my doing," he ground out.

She nodded. "I know. Janet told me later. After I quit the second time—"

After he'd made love with her. If he wasn't so staggered, he'd have pointed out that she had a bad habit of running when things got too personal. But he couldn't feel anything except unrelenting anger.

She leaned back against the counter. "The first time I quit, she convinced me to give it another try."

"Because you owed me," he guessed. The look in her eyes confirmed it.

"I planned to tell you everything when I came back, even though Janet begged me not to. She was hopeful that you were reaching out and said it might be your last chance—"

"Isn't that overly dramatic?"

She shrugged. "I'm just telling you what happened. When I came back inside, I started to thank you and offer my condolences—"

"But you didn't." He would have remembered. One of the things he liked best about her was she'd never said she was sorry. Now he didn't want to like anything about her.

"I didn't because you cut me off. And I realized she was right. If you knew the truth, you'd have shut down. I decided after your body healed I'd—"

"You've had plenty of opportunity to tell me the truth. Why haven't you?"

"I started to care about you, Simon. Not as a nurse for her patient. It scared me. Confused me."

"Did it ever occur to you I might care about you? And this was information I had a right to know?" He took a half step toward her.

"I never wanted this to happen. I only wanted to help you get well." Her hands trembled, spilling coffee. It seeped into the terry cloth covering her, but she didn't notice. "I—I—"

"I was starting to care about you, Megan. And Bayleigh—" He ran his fingers through his hair. "She's something else."

"Yes, she is. And thanks to Marcus—"

"Don't." He held up his hand. "I don't want to hear it. I'm trying to cope with the fact that the little girl of the woman I—'' He'd been about to say *love,* but he couldn't go there. ''She's been looking at me with my son's eyes and you didn't see fit to tell me.''

''Don't take this out on her, Simon.'' For the first time there was fear clouding her eyes. And a protective anger in her voice.

He didn't blame the child. None of this was her fault. In her own way, Bayleigh had told the truth. Her eyes were broken and the doctor fixed them. Simple. And so very complicated. But the fact was, now that he knew, he could never look into that little girl's eyes again without thinking about his son. The sight of her would always be a painful reminder.

Without responding, he walked into the bedroom and quickly dressed. He came out with his suit coat slung over his shoulder and went right past Megan, who hadn't moved from the kitchen.

''Simon?''

He stopped with his hand on the doorknob. ''What?''

''You have every right to be angry with me. I—I deserve it. I don't expect you to believe this, but I really did intend to tell you everything.''

He turned and met her gaze. ''You're right. I don't believe you.''

''I tried to keep you at a distance because I was afraid of this. I did the wrong thing. I admit that. But for the right reason.''

''What's your point, Megan?''

''I've been trying to protect my daughter from being hurt. You pushed your way into our life. You made her love you. But she's innocent. Don't be angry at her.''

He couldn't deny that he was furious—at the whole world. ''This isn't the ER. You can't tell me what to feel.''

"I can tell you what you said." She set her coffee cup on the counter beside her. "You promised Bayleigh you would be at her school play."

"I didn't—"

She walked closer and stopped in front of him, eyes blazing like a mother lion protecting her young. "Don't give me that. In this very room, you told her to count on you. You were going to see her in her costume. This isn't about you and me. This is about a child who's been let down too many times in her short life."

"You should have thought about that before keeping me in the dark."

"To quote you—take me out back and beat the crap out of me. I don't expect you to understand why I did what I did. But I do expect you to be a grown-up. Don't take my sin out on an innocent child."

"How can I get past the fact that your child sees with my child's eyes?"

She ran shaking fingers through her hair. "Using his corneas didn't take his life. And Bayleigh being blind won't bring Marcus back. It's not wrong for me to be grateful for a miracle." Taking a deep breath, she continued, "Bayleigh's father left because she couldn't see. You're leaving because she can. Don't cheapen your son's sacrifice by hanging on to the grieving side of the miracle."

"Don't talk to me about miracles. From where I'm standing it's damn hard to see it that way."

"I know you're angry with me and you've got every right. I didn't mean for you to find out like this. I know it's a shock. But it doesn't change what happened. You've started to live again. You need to move forward with your life."

He opened the door. "I can't, Megan. I'm—"

"Sorry?" she snapped. "How ironic is that coming from you?" She tugged on his arm and made him face her. "The man who doesn't want to hear it."

"Do you have a point?" he asked, sealing his heart off from the anger and pain in her face.

He was being a bastard, and he couldn't help himself. He couldn't believe this was happening. Megan had made him feel again, and he wished he could stop. It hurt so damned much. All he wanted was to get out of there.

"Yeah," she said, "I've got a point. I'm telling you I'm sorry. Sorry I ever met you. And sorry I fell in love with you."

He took one last look, then walked out and closed the door behind him. In spite of everything he'd done to prevent it, he cared again—for Megan. For Bayleigh. He'd begun to think about the idea of being a family.

Thanks to Megan—her deceit, dishonesty, deception—it wasn't going to happen. He felt as if he'd been flattened, like the earth had just caved in.

He'd been living on the edge for two years. Megan had just pushed him over.

Chapter Sixteen

Simon groaned at the knock on his door. He despised himself when hope jumped into his heart that it might be Megan. He couldn't help himself. But it didn't matter who was there. He didn't want to see anyone. He had started downstairs when another loud and agitated round of knocking commenced.

This time it was accompanied by the words, ''Simon, open up. I know you're in there.''

Janet. He could have ignored anyone else, but not her.

He turned the dead bolt and opened the door. ''Make it quick.''

''My sentiments exactly,'' she snapped.

She breezed past him and went inside. Stopping in the center of his living room, she turned to face him. Her short blond hair was tucked behind her ears. He wondered how anyone could look tailored in low-heeled shoes, jeans and a bright yellow sweater set, but Janet managed. She left her purse slung over her shoulder, a hopeful sign this would be quick.

"You look terrible."

"Thank you very much." He rubbed his hand over his chin and winced when the stubble scraped. But there was no reason to shave. "I wasn't expecting company."

"What you mean is you have no excuse to pull yourself together."

"Megan tattled on me."

"I wouldn't call it tattling. She said you finally know the truth. And you're upset with her."

"I'm mad at you, too."

"Simon, you've been mad at me for the past two years. I didn't give up on you then. And like I said before, I'm not giving up on you now."

"What if I've given up on me?"

She lifted her chin and stared at him. "Then you're not the man I thought. You're a coward."

"I can live with that."

Janet nodded, but her brown eyes shimmered with anger. "Living is good. But it's not for the faint of heart."

"What are you talking about?"

"It's best that Megan knows up front who you are. She doesn't need to learn to trust you, then get left in the dust again."

Megan's words came back to him as they had a thousand times in the last week. *He left because she can't see; you're leaving because she can.* Each time he'd remembered, it had taken every ounce of his willpower to keep from going to her. He was angry because he couldn't get her out of his mind, no matter how hard he tried.

"Don't you dare lump me with that guy," he said, lashing out at Janet.

"Why? You're cut from the same cloth. You walked out on her and Bayleigh." She shrugged. "But don't worry about it. She's hurt right now, but I'm sure she'll get over it. She wants a family for her child, and she'll find a man worthy of her who shares the same dream."

Simon wasn't so sure he would get over Megan. He hadn't seen her for seven days and the pain got worse with every one that passed. How could she get past it and go on with someone else? The thought of her with another man was like a knife slicing through his gut.

"If she'd told me up front who she was—"

"You would have shut down faster than Miami under a hurricane warning."

"We'll never know for sure, will we?"

"I know," she said, tapping her chest with a finger.

"You don't know what I'm feeling."

"I know you didn't agree with the decision I made to donate Donna's and Marcus's organs to help others. I'm sorry I robbed you of the opportunity to take the first steps in healing. I deeply regret that. But you were too far away. The window of time for viable transplant is too small. And I will never regret helping others live. I hope they're as blessed as we were by their lives."

"My son is dead."

"If I could change that, don't you think I would? But I found a way to make sense of something I couldn't change. Every year, nearly five thousand people die while waiting on transplant lists for organs that could save their lives. We didn't get a choice about whether or not Donna and Marcus lived. But we did get a choice about helping some of those people *not* to die. Or giving children like Bayleigh a better quality of life."

"But her life wasn't in danger—"

"Would she have died without the surgery? No. If I'd

withheld consent to donate Marcus's corneas would it have saved him? No. It was the only way to make some sense of it, to find a positive, something good to come out of an unimaginably horrific situation.''

''And you think it's a wonder?''

''I think it's a miracle.''

Megan had said the same thing. ''I understand what you're saying intellectually. But I can't help thinking—''

''Megan's daughter can see and you begrudge that.''

''No. Megan lied to me about the fact that her daughter can see with my son's eyes. She should have told me up front—''

''I told her not to.''

He blinked. ''She said that. But I didn't believe—'' Because he'd opened up, accepted her. Fallen for her. Now it hurt like hell. ''How could you do this to me?''

''How could I not?'' She held out her hands. ''For the first time in two years, I had a smidgeon of hope for you. I had to take a chance. And, for the record, she didn't want to do it. I'm still not sure why she went along with the program. But it worked. You've joined the living again. You're in love with her.''

''That's crazy.'' He folded his arms over his chest. ''I don't care—''

''Baloney. You care too much. About Bayleigh. And Megan.''

''I care that she lied to me.''

''The truth is you're relieved that she didn't tell you up front.''

''Now you're scaring me.''

''Come on, Simon. It's as clear as the fact that you're in love with her. You call it lying, but she didn't misrepresent anything. At most she left out details. In reality she did you a favor.''

"A favor?"

"If you can convince yourself she's a dishonorable person, you've got an excuse to feel superior when you turn your back on her and Bayleigh. That makes you better than the man who walked out on her and his child. He split because he couldn't deal with the problems of an imperfect child. You're running away because you love them both. And you're scared to care about someone that much again."

He couldn't deny what she was saying. "What about the fact that every time I look at Bayleigh, I'll see Marcus? I'll remember—"

"That a business trip came up on a weekend you were supposed to spend with him?"

He winced. "Not a day has passed in two years that I didn't wish I could go back and do it over."

"And when you look at Bayleigh you'll see that? Instead of her beautiful little face? Or her sweet smile? Or the sound of her laughter? Or her contagious enthusiasm?"

"How can I not think about Marcus?" he said, desperate for her to give him the answer.

"We'll never forget Marcus. He was a wonderful, bright little boy. We'll always think about him and love him."

Simon felt tears burn his eyes. "Will it ever stop hurting?"

"No." She shook her head. "But it will become bearable." She moved toward him and put her hand on his arm. "You wouldn't be the man I admire if you didn't feel things so deeply. But the sadness will ease and you'll remember only the good times. You *should* think about your son and be grateful a part of him lives on in this child. You should think about him and, instead of the guilt, remind yourself that if not for Marcus, Bayleigh wouldn't be able to see how much you love her mother."

He felt as if she'd whacked him over the head with a two-by-four. But his gut told him she was right. About everything. "Oh, God—"

Janet smiled then hugged him. "Now stop this nonsense. Quit wallowing in guilt and go tell Megan how much you love her and that adorable child of hers."

"You don't pull punches, do you?" he asked, one corner of his mouth lifting.

She just smiled. "Go shave. You look dreadful, and I won't have Bayleigh frightened."

Then she kissed his cheek and walked out the front door.

He loved Megan. He'd known from the first, and part of him had been running from the truth ever since. Because he *was* afraid of caring again. That was no excuse for letting down the two most important ladies in his life. He'd made mistakes, but he could only try to do better in the future. Bravery wasn't the absence of fear. Heroes moved forward in spite of it. He was no hero, but he refused to be a coward any longer.

He was finally at peace with the past. He could live with it now. What he couldn't live with was the way he'd hurt Megan. Somehow, he had to make things right—with her and her child. She and Bayleigh were a package deal.

They were his future.

"Mommy, where's Simon?"

Bayleigh glanced past Megan to the doorway of her classroom, looking for a man who wasn't going to be there. He hadn't come right out and said so, but she knew. The little girl had asked about him every day, a hundred times a day, ever since he'd walked out of their lives forever.

"Sweetie, I don't think he's coming."

"But he promised," she said, her mouth trembling. "He wanted to see me in my costume. It's not bad luck now."

It's bad luck your mother is an idiot, she wanted to say.

The kindergarten holiday production was just about to start. Only parents were allowed in the classroom to help with last-minute costume adjustments. Scaled-down desks and child-sized chairs filled the center area and kiddie artwork decorated the walls. The room was bustling with adorable children dressed as angels and other characters for the play about a long-ago miracle. It would take a modern miracle to fix Bayleigh's broken heart.

Megan sat in a tiny chair so she could look her daughter in the eyes. "You know he's got a job now, Bay. He probably got tied up with work." He probably lit candles in gratitude that he wouldn't be stuck with her.

The little girl's big blue eyes brimmed with tears before she stared down at the pink-trimmed sneakers peeking out from beneath the hem of her white dress. "I thought he liked me a little. I thought maybe—"

With her knuckle, Megan nudged Bayleigh's chin up. "What, sweetie?"

"I thought he might want to be my dad."

"Oh, baby—"

Megan bit the inside of her lip to keep back the sob. If she ever saw him again, she was going to give him a gravel extracting he would never forget. He could be as mad at her as he wanted. She deserved it. But that did *not* give him the right to hurt this child.

As much as she wanted to pin all the blame on him,

it wasn't entirely his fault. She should have told him the truth right away. She knew better than to get so personally involved with a patient. But somehow, with Simon, it had been personal from the first moment she'd seen him. And she'd tried so hard to keep him at arm's length but nothing had worked.

She'd harbored a small hope that he would show up tonight. Not for her. For Bayleigh. She realized now her hope was selfish, and she'd yearned to see him again. If only for a moment. To give him a piece of her mind. It was all she had left after giving him her heart.

"Simon likes you more than a little." Megan took her daughter's small hands into her own. "But he still misses his own little boy."

"Maybe he wouldn't miss him so much if he had a little girl." Behind her glasses, Bayleigh's blue eyes were tragic and hopeful all at the same time.

Megan couldn't bear to see the yearning for what could never be. What a mess she'd made of both their lives. She fussed with the angel costume, straightening the wings Simon had engineered, then attached to the long-sleeved white satin dress her mother had made. He'd fashioned a halo from leftover scraps and Megan fiddled with it, making sure it was upright. Bayleigh's golden hair gleamed in the overhead fluorescent lights.

"You know Grammy and Grampy are already in their seats in the auditorium, saving a place for me. They can't wait to see how you look."

"Children, it's time to line up." The teacher stood in the front of the room. "We have to go on in fifteen minutes."

Following her directive, there was a flurry of noise as parents guided their little ones into the line and, with one last fond, nervous look, left.

"It's time for me to go." Megan gave Bayleigh a hug and kiss. "Knock 'em dead, sweetie." She felt someone behind her as she released her child.

The little girl stepped back, looked up and squealed, "Simon!" She squeezed past the chair and threw herself at his legs. "You're here."

Megan turned to see him. She couldn't look at him hard enough. She was so sure he wouldn't show up. At the same time she was so angry at him she couldn't see straight.

He went down on one knee and pulled Bayleigh into his arms. "Hey, kiddo. You look like an angel."

She giggled. "That's what I'm s'posed to be, silly. Mommy said maybe you had to work, but I knew you'd come."

"I had some things to work through," he said, looking at Megan. "But I'm here now. Nothing comes before family. I just wanted to say hi. You better go get in line now."

"Okay," she said, nodding.

"I saw your grandparents. They're saving seats." He straightened the halo again. "I'll be up front. Right beside your mom."

She nodded and started to follow the other children, then she threw herself against him. "I love you, Simon."

"I love you, too."

The sight of Bayleigh's golden head and his dark one so close together squeezed Megan's heart and churned up all the tenderness inside it. She had a lump the size of a grapefruit in her throat.

Bayleigh looked him in the eyes and said, "I'll try to help you not miss your little boy."

He swallowed hard. "I'd like that very much," he answered in a deep, husky voice.

"If you love me and I love you does that mean you're my dad?"

"That's up to your mom."

"Bayleigh, it's time to get in line," the teacher reminded her gently.

Simon tapped her nose. "You're going to get left behind. Break a leg."

"Huh?"

"That means good luck."

Megan's chest hurt, and she couldn't think of a single cardiac medication that would help. She couldn't seem to draw enough air into her lungs. And, most of all, she wanted to cry.

"See you later, Simon."

"Count on it."

Then Bayleigh hurried off, following the three wise men as they lined up with the other children in costume. Their teacher led them from the room and a couple of parents followed. Then she was alone with Simon in a kindergarten classroom.

"Hi." He stood, then glanced over his shoulder at the empty doorway. "She looks great."

"Yeah. I didn't think you'd come," she said, standing, too.

"I had a visit from a wise woman."

"I didn't know Janet would go to see you. I just thought she should know that you knew—well, you know."

"I know." His mouth tilted up at the corners. "A while back she told me I was living in perpetual midnight. That darkness and gloom were my best friends."

"Sounds like Janet."

"And would you like to know what else this wise woman said to me?"

"Yes?" She looked up at him, unable to read the expression in his eyes. "No? Maybe?"

"After she finished beating the crap out of me—verbally speaking," he clarified, "she said I love you."

"Janet loves you?"

He laughed. "No. Well, yes, but not that way. I'm botching this so badly." He ran a hand through his hair. "Why is it so hard with the most important things?"

"I'm not exactly sure what you're trying to say. But I have something you need to hear. After that, you may not want to say any more."

"Okay." He stuck his hands in his pockets.

He looked good—plaid sport shirt, brown slacks, coordinating jacket. Casual. Wonderful. She'd been nervous when she first saw him. Now, she felt like the condemned with nothing to lose.

Her chin lifted as she met his gaze. "Bayleigh let you off the hook because she's only five. She was easy. I'm not. You made her love you. You promised to be here, and she thought you weren't coming. If you'd spoiled this for her—how dare you do that to her?"

"You couldn't possibly know—"

"Don't tell me I don't understand. I know you've been to hell and back. Maybe I should have told you the truth right away. I didn't. That's my mistake. But it doesn't give you the right to hurt my child. You insinuated yourself into our lives—in spite of my objections. That comes with responsibilities. Top of the list is not breaking promises."

"If anyone understands that, I do," he said solemnly. "It's why I'm here. That and the fact I admire you more than you can possibly know. Protecting and defending Bayleigh above everything. That's the way it should be. I know better than anyone."

"Protect and defend? Sounds like LAPD." Her bubble of fury was beginning to lose air. That was bad. As soon as it was gone the pain would hit.

"Megan, you're absolutely right. I handled it badly. My only excuse is—" He sighed. "I have no excuse. There is no good reason for hurting Bayleigh. I swear it will never happen again. And I hope you'll accept my apology."

The mad disappeared. Gone. Poof. An aching sadness with overtones of pain filled her from the pit of her stomach all the way to her heart.

She nodded. "Forget it, Simon. I have to go find my seat now." She started to slide past him.

"Wait. There's one more thing I have to say." He took her hands in his. "The last time I saw you—when you said you were sorry you love me, did you mean it?"

"That I love you? Or that I was sorry?"

"Never mind." He sighed. "I just want to say I love you. And I will never, ever be sorry."

That did it. The tears she'd been trying desperately to hold back overflowed and trickled down her cheeks.

Concern darkened his eyes. "Don't cry. Please. I hate myself for hurting you like this. I promise, if you'll give me another chance, I'll make it up to you."

"No. I need—"

He shook his head. "Don't you dare tell me that. I know I haven't given you any reason to trust me. But I swear I'm not like him. I won't turn my back on you and Bayleigh when you need me most. Not now. Not ever." His grip on her hands tightened almost painfully as dark intensity glowed in his eyes.

"It's not that. I know you're not like him." She shook her head. "I didn't mean no. I meant finding out the way you did was a shock. As much as I'd like to, I can't blame you for being angry with me."

"I'm not mad. I'm an idiot. But I'm finally at peace with the past. Or maybe it took you to get through to me. To give me a reason to live, to love, to take a chance again." He stared into her eyes and myriad emotions swirled in his own. "But if you can't forgive me—"

"Of course I can. I love you."

"As simple as that?"

"Of course it's not. I want to stay mad. You're not the only one afraid to take a chance, you know."

"I know." He cupped her face in his hands, brushing the moisture from her cheeks with his thumbs. "But what else can you do when you love someone?"

Megan's eyes drifted closed. When his lips grazed hers in a sweet kiss, she couldn't suppress a sigh of utter contentment.

Then she looked at him. "So where do two cowards go from here?"

"All the way," he said. "Simon says marry me."

Her eyes widened. "You don't waste any time."

"I've wasted too much time already. Waiting won't make it any more right. You're a moonlight kind of gal, and I've waited my whole life for you. I love you and I want to be Bayleigh's father. The question is—can you trust me to do that?"

She smiled through her tears. "Absolutely."

"How can you be so sure?"

"A man who grieves as deeply as you is capable of love in direct proportion. That's a whole lotta love." She nodded. "There's not a question in my mind. Bayleigh would be a lucky little girl to have you for her father."

"Does that go for husbands, too? Because I want more

than anything to be yours. I promise to spend the rest of my life making both of you happy. What do you say?''

''I say we'd be fools to turn our backs on this miracle. I say, yes, I'll marry you.''

He grinned and her knees went weak. ''Then Nurse Brightwell, I think we should seal the bargain with some serious mouth-to-mouth resuscitation.''

''Okay. And I've always wanted to say this—kiss me, you fool.''

And he did.

After existing in midnight, moonlight and miracles were the very best medicine.

* * * * *

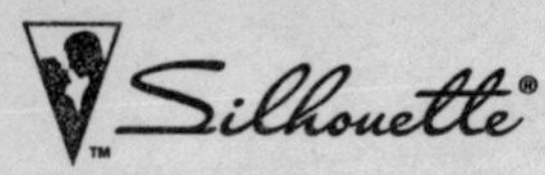

SPECIAL EDITION®

COMING NEXT MONTH

#1519 HER HEALING TOUCH—Lindsay McKenna
Morgan's Mercenaries: Destiny's Women
Angel Paredes, a paramedic in the Peruvian Army, was known for her legendary powers of healing but could not heal her own wounded heart. When she was paired with handsome Special Forces Officer Burke Gifford for a life-threatening mission, she discovered love was the true healer, and that Burke was the only one who could save her....

#1520 COMPLETELY SMITTEN—Susan Mallery
Hometown Heartbreakers
When preacher's daughter and chronic good-girl Haley Foster was all but dumped by her fiancé, she took off on a road trip, determined to change her people-pleasing ways. Kevin Harmon, a reformed bad boy and U.S. Marshal wound up right in the middle of Haley's plans. Was it possible that these two opposites could end up completely smitten?

#1521 A FATHER'S FORTUNE—Shirley Hailstock
Erin Taylor loved children, but she'd long ago given up on having a family of her own—until she hired James "Digger" Clayton to renovate her day-care center. One smile at a time, this brawny builder was reshaping her heart.... Could she convince him to try his hand at happily-ever-after?

#1522 THERE GOES THE BRIDE—Crystal Green
Kane's Crossing
When full-figured ex-beauty queen Daisy Cox left her cheating groom at the altar, Rick Shane piloted her to safety. The love-wary ex-soldier only planned to rescue a damsel-in-distress, never realizing that he might fall for this runaway bride!

#1523 WEDDING OF THE CENTURY—Patricia McLinn
You could say Annette Trevetti and Steve Corbett had a history together. Seven years ago, their wedding was interrupted by Steve's ex-girlfriend—carrying a baby she claimed was his! Annette left town promptly, then returned years later to find Steve a single father to another man's child. Was their love strong enough to overcome their past misunderstanding?

#1524 FAMILY MERGER—Leigh Greenwood
Ron Egan was a high-powered businessman who learned that no amount of money could solve all his problems. For suddenly his sixteen-year-old daughter was pregnant, and in a home for unwed mothers. Kathryn Roper, who ran the home, agreed to help Ron reconnect with his daughter—and maybe make a connection of their own....

SSECNM0103